A Christmas Match

Pam Binder

A Canadian Christmas

Darcy Carson

A Saucy Christmas

DeeAnna Galbraith

A Collection of Sweet and Sensual Christmas Romances

written by

Pam Binder

Darcy Carson

DeeAnna Galbraith

Edited, arranged, and published by

Reads Publishing

Contact information: Pam Binder, pambinder.com, Darcy Carson, darcycarsonbooks.com, and DeeAnna Galbraith, deeannagalbraith.com

Cover art by Angela Carson

Print ISBN: 978-1-7350188-2-9

Digital ISBN: 978-1-7350188-3-6

A Christmas Match

Pam Binder

Chapter One

Coincidence is just another word for Magic

A car alarm screeched in protest as the sidewalk rolled under Melody McBride's feet where she stood across from the Second Chance restaurant and Kirkland Marina. She steadied herself with the skill she'd acquired as a rock climber and waited for the earthquake tremor to subside. She said a silent prayer that this was naturally occurring and not a sign that her aunts had resumed old habits. They had been warned repeatedly. Another infraction and they would lose their matchmaking license.

The windows at the restaurant and the newly renovated boutique hotel rattled in response to the earthquake, then quieted as the ground calmed as quickly as it had erupted. A middle-aged couple dressed in matching Christmas sweaters and loaded down with packages exited the hotel in a hurry. Their expressions reminded Melody of deer caught in the headlights of an oncoming truck. Melody could relate. She'd had that feeling most of her life.

"It's just a minor Seattle tremor," Melody said with a smile, hoping to calm the couple as she bent to pick up a canvas tote bag the woman had dropped. Across the red canvas bag were the words, I Heart Seattle. "It's over now. We get them all the time."

The husband mouthed a thank you as he dialed for a taxi.

The woman accepted the tote with a smile that lit up her rosy cheeks. "You're such a sweety and cute as a button." She hugged the tote bag against her chest as her smile broadened. "I would have forgotten I dropped it, and it's stuffed with presents for my grandchildren. I even bought a few things for Tom's son, Billy." She winked. "We're one of those blended families. Billy's not married yet, but we are hopeful. He is such a nice boy and like most his age, works all the time and too busy to find the perfect woman." She hugged the tote tighter and lowered her voice. "That's why we're staying here. We had an appointment with the matchmakers. Are you single?"

Her husband eased the tote from his wife's grasp. "I'm sure the young woman doesn't want to know why we're here, DeDe, and I'm even more certain that if she doesn't already have a special someone, she has a steady stream of suitors. Besides, our taxi has arrived, and we must leave or we'll miss our plane. Thank you again, miss…"

"Melody McBride."

DeDe glanced toward her husband. "Melody has the same last name as the aunts. She must be the niece they were talking about. The one who's wasting her life."

Tom's eyebrows knitted together in a frown. "My apologies, Melody. DeDe has a way of blurting out things."

DeDe kissed Tom on the check. "Like the time I told you I loved you and asked you to marry me."

Tom's grin broadened and his eyes sparkled with love. "I'd been trying all day to get up the courage to ask you."

DeDe kissed Tom again and turned toward Melody. "I shouldn't have said what I did, though. I'm sure I misunderstood."

Melody forced a smile. "No worries." She wanted to defend herself and tell Tom and DeDe that her aunts were mistaken. She wasn't wasting her life: she had just put it on hold. Instead of contradicting her aunts, she held the taxi door open, keeping her smile in place.

Tom nodded his thanks as he and DeDe piled into the taxi and rode away. They were such a cute couple, so in love and so caring toward each other. When she encountered couples like Tom and DeDe, Melody always thought of her parents. She was convinced that if they had lived, that their love would have continued to glow as brightly. Her three aunts had raised her after her parents had died in a car crash when she was a sophomore in high school.

She swept away the heavy feeling that always settled over her when she thought about her parents and entered the café.

The last time she'd been here was over Thanksgiving. Fall decorations had been replaced by Christmas greens, reds, and golds, complete with a Christmas tree as the centerpiece of the café. Their cat, Charmer, meowed a hello, with an edge of judgment as though to say that it had been too long since Melody's last visit. She rubbed the silver cat behind his floppy ears. He always reminded Melody of the description of the owl in the Harry Potter books. Despite the cat's judgmental tone, she gave him a kiss on the top of his head and scanned the café for her aunts.

The café was humming with activity this morning, and Melody recognized most of the customers as regulars. There was the retired couple who lived in the apartment building a few blocks away, mothers with baby strollers who'd stopped in for their morning lattés, and a handful of joggers who made the café their last stop. No one seemed to have been bothered by the tremor, which only added to Melody's suspicion. If there had been an earthquake, why had only the elderly couple felt it? Had her aunts wanted Melody to run into them?

Her aunts were clustered around a small table, sipping tea, eating pastries, and looking as calm and innocent as harbor seals basking in the afternoon sun. They were like precious gemstones in the setting of a crown: Cassy always wore green, Isadora blue, and Shawna red, and all three glowed as though they were lit from within. The only thing that changed was their hairstyles. Today all three wore their salt and pepper hair piled on their heads in matronly buns as though wanting to be taken seriously. But the severity of their hairstyles only accentuated the glitter eyeshadow they wore that matched their clothes.

But something was wrong. She could sense it in the air.

She nodded hello to the newest hire for the holiday season, who was working behind the counter making lattés. Ginger was on scholarship at the University of Washington and was majoring in hotel management. But Melody knew it wasn't the young woman's impressive credentials that had landed her the temporary job. Or because her hair was spiky and the color of pink cotton candy and her heart-shaped face resembled the fairy figurines the aunts sold in the gift shop. Ginger's father had died in combat in the Middle East and with three younger siblings, Ginger and her mother were having a tough time making ends meet. Melody didn't know how her aunts had found out about Ginger, but once they had, they had taken both Ginger and her family under their wing.

The realization of how many people like her and Ginger her aunts had helped softened the confrontational speech Melody was planning. But as she headed to the aunts' table, she saw the cause of her unease. Isadora's leg was propped on a chair on a cushion of pillows with her ankle taped, and Aunt Shawna's right arm was in a sling.

Melody rushed over. "What happened? And why didn't you call me?"

Aunty Cassy handed Melody a scone. "It all happened late last night. We were carrying boxes of decorations down the stairs, and Charmer scampered under our feet. One thing led to another, and we all came tumbling down like Jack and Jill. I just have a few bruises, but Shawna and Isadora were not as lucky. And then we were so busy this morning, we forgot to call."

Melody pulled up a chair next to Aunty Cassy. "Are you sure you're okay?"

"Positive. But the timing could not have been worse. We are expected to help with the Campbell wedding this afternoon at Lake Union. It's one of those destination weddings that have become the rage. It starts at Lake Union with the rehearsal dinner while cruising to Victoria, British Columbia. The wedding party will tour Victoria and the Butchart Gardens and return during the Christmas Festival of Ships Parade where the bride and groom will marry. It's all very romantic but a lot of work coordinating. I can't do it on my own, and our new hire is needed here."

Melody squeezed Aunty Cassy's hand. "I'll be glad to help. Victoria, B.C. isn't that far from Seattle. I am presuming it's overnight. I'll let my boss know at the camping store. He won't be happy. This is our busiest time of the year."

Aunty Isadora handed Melody a latté. "We knew we could rely on you to help. Actually, it takes place over three nights."

Melody accepted the latté they had preordered for her. "I can make that happen. I have vacation time building up dust bunnies. I'll let my boss know, go home and pack, and meet you at Lake Union this afternoon." She eyed her aunts. They were the most loving and generous people she had ever known and always looked sweet and innocent, but she couldn't shake the feeling they were up to something. She had also learned that when she had this feeling it was best to approach her questioning in a roundabout way. She started with the couple and the suspicious earthquake.

She leaned forward, keeping her voice low. "Aunty Cassy, I told a nice couple that the earthquake was minor. Did you all have anything to do with it?"

Aunty Isadora peered over her sapphire-blue reading glasses. "Why do you think we're involved?"

Melody reached over to Aunty Isadora's cup and grabbed the spoon that was spinning in a circle on its own, like the scene in the movie *Practical Magic* with Sandra Bullock. "Wild guess."

Aunty Isadora shrugged. "I was excited. We haven't seen you in over a month."

"You can't be mad," Aunty Shawna added.

Aunty Cassy licked chocolate from her fingers. "Shawna is right. We are getting old and sometimes things just happen. You did a wonderful job with the Elizabeth Sanders and Eric O'Shay wedding, dear. You have a gift."

Melody recognized the ploy to change the subject. Her aunts never wanted to discuss what they referred to as their "little accidents." She reached for her coffee drink that was now stone cold. She drank some anyway. "You may have fooled some people that you are losing your touch, but this is me. What are you up to? Are you staging a comeback?"

"Only if you'll join us," Aunty Cassy said.

Melody scraped her chair back from the table. "We've talked about this before. I am content working at the camping store. I get great discounts on hiking equipment, and the people are nice. Besides, I'd make a terrible matchmaker. Love does not last. Stuff happens. You are the ones who believe in love at first sight, not me. And believing in happily-ever-afters is a key component of matchmaking."

"Your parents believed in love at first sight," Aunty Isadora said.

Melody looked away. "That was a different time. Love is more complicated now. People must have things in common, similar goals, backgrounds, and aspirations."

"You're talking about the qualities needed if you are organizing a group hike to Mount Everest," Aunty Shawna said. "Love doesn't follow rules or lists. Love is messy, unpredictable, and full of surprises."

Aunty Isadora nodded. "Speaking of love, how is it progressing with that nice man you introduced to us a few months ago? Ted. Ned… Does he still want to marry you?"

"Fred was his name, and you hated him."

Aunty Cassy reached out and squeezed Melody's hand. "We didn't hate him, dear. We just thought you could do better."

"Well, so did he. He found someone else and broke up with me last week in a text message."

Aunty Cassy frowned. "I'm so sorry. Are you all right?"

Melody slipped her hand from her aunt's. "I'm fine. It really wasn't that unexpected. We never made time for each other and even when we were together there weren't any sparks. Don't worry about me. Now, I must go. Be good."

"Why be good when you can be great?" Aunty Isadora said, smiling.

Melody mirrored the smile and leaned over to give Aunty Isadora a hug. The saying was her mother's and Melody appreciated that the aunts had made sure the memory of her parents was kept alive. "I love you all." Melody glanced at her cellphone to check the time. "I am late for work. I'll finish my shift and then go home and pack."

"Of course, dear," Aunty Shawna said. "Just curious. Would you like a real prince in your life now that what's-his-name is out of the picture?"

"Who wouldn't?" Melody said over her shoulder as she rushed from the café.

Chapter Two

Silence hovered over the café and seemed to hold its breath as the door closed behind Melody. In the next instant, as though someone had flipped a switch, the latté machine swished to life.

Cassy felt her blood pressure rise. "Shawna, why in the world would you ask Melody that question?" But Shawna and Isadora had left the table and were headed toward the window that faced the street.

Cassy rose from the table, more tired than she had been in days. Lying to her niece did not sit well. There had not been an accident on the stairs, and she hated blaming Charmer for the fabricated fall. Charmer would never do such a thing. He knew better. She would make sure she gave him an extra treat and apologize profusely. But she was desperate.

She crossed to the cupboard against the wall where she displayed her collection of Belleek china with its signature Irish Shamrock design and where she stored her tins of tea. She needed to keep busy. It was true that her plan had worked, and

Melody had agreed to help her with the wedding, but the bigger issue remained. Cassy was worried about her niece. Melody had never let go of the guilt she felt over her parents' car accident. They had all been working late that night, and instead of driving back with them, Melody had stayed to finish decorating the inside of a boat her father hoped to sell.

Cassy packed two tins of her favorite Irish Breakfast tea in her embroidered tote bag and added a tin with a variety of herbal teas for good measure. The destination wedding to Victoria she'd planned for King Campbell and his fiancée was scheduled to take place over two nights. But experience had taught her to expect the unexpected and always be prepared. She didn't want to run out of her tea and resort to whatever passed for tea on the yacht. The Campbells were from New Zealand so she assumed they would carry a supply of English tea, and if there was one thing that she could not abide it was drinking English tea.

She set her tote bag aside and settled at the table to finish her tea and scone. "Shawna, please move away from the window. Melody will see you. You are supposed to have your arm in a sling, remember?"

"Melody is in her car. She cannot see me. Do you think her comment that she'd like a prince gives us permission to go forward with our plan?"

"Close enough. She is stubborn. In the past she made it quite clear she is not interested in our matchmaking services, and when she is ready, she'll find someone on her own."

Isadora harrumphed and jogged over to the window. "Melody is more interested in finding someone who sounds good on paper than trusting her heart. She does not believe in love. You know her track record. She picks the man of the moment, not the man of forever-after. We must do something and fast. That horrible man who broke up with her had a change of heart after he discovered the amount of her inheritance. He plans to ask her to marry him."

Cassy set her tea down so hard the cup rattled on the saucer. "How do you know this, and why wasn't I told?

Isadora refilled Cassy's tea. "You were out walking Charmer when what's-his-face arrived this morning, and then we were busy with customers. There wasn't time."

Cassy sipped her tea, concentrating on the breakfast blend to sooth her nerves. "What did he want?"

"He had the audacity to ask if we had a family engagement ring we could give him for Melody."

"You didn't give him great-Grandmother's did you?"

"Of course not," Shawna said. "But he's persistent. Are you sure our plan will work?"

Cassy shook her head. "Nothing is certain. All we can do is present the possibility."

"And of course if it doesn't work," Shawna said, "Melody will be furious."

"It's worth the risk," Isadora said. "Where do we start?"

Cassy finished her tea and motioned for Ginger. She would need to fill Ginger in on a few details if their plan were to work. "We start with a handsome prince."

Chapter Three

Prince William Campbell IV operated the bridge and main control center of his family's power yacht, the *Royal Escape*, as he maneuvered the vessel past the Ballard Locks of Seattle, Washington, and made his way to Lake Union. He had not veered off course once since leaving New Zealand, although there had been times when he would have preferred to bypass Puget Sound and turn around and return home. This was the worst time for him to be gone. Two-thirds of the way into this trip, he received news that one of the cattle on their ranch had been found dead, and he was waiting for the toxicology report.

But he had made a promise to his father and King. His father was remarrying after being a widower for over twenty years. William wanted to believe this would make his father happy, but William was worried. Everything had happened so fast. One minute his father had seemed content to govern their timber empire in New Zealand, and the next he had announced he was marrying and relinquishing his crown and duties. His father had never been impulsive and resisted change in every aspect of his life, from choosing the color of a suit to implementing innovative measures for harvesting the forest.

William had never met the woman his father intended to marry and researching her name had resulted in a dead end. Until he understood the woman's motives, William intended to do everything in his power to delay the wedding.

His first officer, Ben Perdy, entered the bridge, perched his glasses on his shaved head, and rubbed his eyes. The man was a weathered seaman, confirmed bachelor, and had hired on as a deckhand when William's father had been captain. William was grateful Officer Perdy had agreed to accompany him on this voyage and Perdy was as confused as William regarding the King's impulsive behavior.

Officer Perdy yawned. "Thanks for letting me sleep. Chef Coffee kept me up half the night. The man might be the best cook on the seven seas, but he has been in an odd place and he's a loose cannon. He swore he would jump ship when we docked if we allowed the wedding planner to take over his galley. I didn't know what to tell him. The last time we had a wedding on board was when your parents married, and your mother made all the arrangements. She was quite a woman."

William tamped down the warm nostalgia that pervaded him whenever his mother was mentioned. Although she had died of cancer when he was barely out of short pants, his memories were still vivid and painful. People advised him that talking about her would ease the pain. He disagreed.

He forced the memories back down and peered out the window on the bridge. The sky darkened and rain slashed across the window, promising a stormy day. He checked his instruments and slowed the yacht, preparing to dock. His father and his fiancée were in Victoria B.C. and expected to arrive that afternoon by float plane, and he wanted everything in place before they arrived.

"I will talk with Coffee when we dock. If all goes as planned there won't be a wedding, and I can take the first plane back to New Zealand."

Officer Perdy nodded, coming up alongside William. "I understand your concern regarding your father. But I think it's different this time." The man hesitated, leaning closer to the window. "Is that a woman standing out in the rain?"

William followed Officer Perdy's line of vision. Sure enough, a woman stood not far from the location where he planned to moor the yacht. Her long hair whipped in the frozen wind, and her coat flapped behind her like a cape, yet her stance was defiant as though challenging the elements. She reminded him of the stories his mother had told him of the warrior goddesses of New Zealand and the South Pacific. She was magnificent.

Chapter Four

Melody was on hold, freezing and buffed around by an icy wind that blew over the water of Lake Union. Surrounded by her luggage and boxes of decorations, she stood her ground. She stood on a pier not far from a museum dedicated to wooden boats and the maritime history of the Pacific Northwest. The afternoon's weather had turned bipolar. One minute the sun peeked out from behind the clouds, and the next it went into hiding as a gust of wind blew in from the north.

And to make matters more frustrating she was on hold, listening to the movie soundtrack of *Sleepless in Seattle*. When it came around a third time to the song When I Fall in Love by Celine Dion, and then A Kiss to Build a Dream On by Louis Armstrong, her patience was reaching its limit.

Her aunts had the background information on their client, King Thomas Campbell, and Melody only knew the yacht's name was *Royal Escape* and was expected today. The name of the boat told her everything she needed to know about its owner. From the tabloids she had surmised that members of the royal hereditary families of the world thought they had it rough. But what did they have to escape from? Their choices seemed to range from what designer dress they should wear to what island should they buy next.

The steady rain turned to ice and dumped from the grey sky. She shivered as a ginormous yacht—she estimated it at over one hundred feet—docked a short distance away. She suspected it might be the *Royal Escape*, but she couldn't very well march up to its captain and announce that she was the wedding planner. That was unprofessional. And would they even believe her?

She lost the connection on her cellphone.

"Seriously?" She punched in the number to her aunts' café again. Her Aunty Cassy was late. She was supposed to have been here thirty minutes ago to help make the introductions.

Their new assistant answered with an annoyingly cheery voice. "Thank you for calling the Second Chance Café and Bed and Breakfast. May I put you on hold?"

"No, don't put me on…"

The call went directly to the song *Stardust* by Nat King Cole.

The sky darkened as Melody huffed a sigh, cradled her cellphone against her ear, and knelt to search for her umbrella in her suitcase. She tore through clothes she had tossed from her closet and dresser into her suitcase in a haphazard fashion. There were mismatched shoes, a pair of summer slacks, lingerie, a slinky black dress she'd bought for a date with Fred but hadn't worn because he had cancelled, sweats…

A dark shadow hovered over her, blocking out the icy rain and wind.

"Is this yours?" A man stood beside her holding a giant black umbrella over her head in one hand and dangling a red bra in the other.

Eyes as green as a summer sea held her in their gaze. His skin was bronzed by the wind and sun, and it looked like he hadn't shaved in days. She swallowed, shivering again.

He squatted, bringing the umbrella closer as his features turned concerned. "You are cold. Are you waiting for someone?" His voice held a slight accent, not quite British, but close.

Her heart leapt to her throat and wanted to shout – *I've been waiting for you.*

She ordered her libido under control, snatched the bra from him, and stuffed it into her coat pocket. "Yes, thank you." She concentrated on stuffing her clothes back into her suitcase. She'd caught only a glimpse of him, but he was gorgeous. Not in that Greek god or movie-star/model way, but rugged with broad shoulders in the "Me Tarzan, you Jane" way. Updated version of course, where sometimes Tarzan saves Jane and sometimes Jane saves Tarzan. "Whoa. Slow down."

"I beg your pardon?" the man said.

"Ramblings of a person suffering from hyperthermia." She shook her head and zipped her suitcase.

"You should come inside with me, then. My boat just docked." He reached for her suitcase and turned as though the matter were settled.

She hurried to catch up and stay under the umbrella. "You're from the *Royal Escape*?"

His sidelong glance turned her chilled blood warm and fuzzy. "I am."

"Prefect. I'm here to meet with the captain."

He stopped abruptly as his gaze lost its warmth. "Who are you?"

Making a good impression had always been Melody's strong suit. According to her ex-boyfriend, it was when they got to know her that she became prickly. She drew on her strength as she thought of happy things, like videos of kittens and puppies, and held her hand toward the tall man with a scowl on his face.

"I'm Melody McBride, the wedding planner," she said in a rush to his deepening frown. "Well, actually, I'm helping my aunts as two of them aren't feeling well. One broke her arm, and the other a leg. They claimed it was a silly accident, but I'm still not sure what happened." She made her voice lighter as though she wasn't worried. She took a breath. "Anyway, and you are?"

"Prince William Campbell IV"

She hadn't seen that coming, but as soon as she announced who she was and he had told her his name, his demeanor had changed. She wasn't sure she liked this version. She summoned her professional voice and pasted on a smile. "Your father is the lucky bridegroom."

"It would seem so."

His voice was as frosty as the air, and she heard the disapproval loud and clear. Her aunts had said that when a child's parent remarried, regardless of the reason, it could be like paddling a boat up stream with a fork.

The rain and sleet continued to dump from the sky, ignoring the fact that she was drenched to the skin and freezing. Mr. Prince, upon finding out who she was, hadn't invited her onboard his floating palace. Was the man rude or was something else going on?

She plunged forward in a manufactured cheery voice as though things weren't awkward. "I'm expecting my aunt shortly, but I'd love to board your boat and start setting up the decorations. We are short-staffed and have a lot to do before the wedding guests arrive."

"You are not what I expected." As impossible as it seemed, the man's scowl deepened. "You are fired." He hesitated, then thrust the umbrella into her hand. "You may keep the umbrella." With that announcement he turned on his heels and jogged the short distance to the *Royal Escape* and boarded his yacht.

Chapter Five

Icy rain pelted on the umbrella, giving Melody a headache that threatened to morph into a full-blown migraine. What had just happened?

Aunty Cassy came up alongside Melody and deposited Charmer on the ground. She wore a neon yellow waterproof hat and matching, ankle-length rain jacket. She looked dressed to brave the storms in the Gulf of Alaska, not take a leisurely, half-day cruise to Victoria, B.C. "I'm sorry I'm late. Charmer insisted on coming along and it took me a while to find his chew toy."

Melody held the umbrella over her aunt's head. "We were just fired."

She shook away the fog from her brain at the Prince's announcement and only half-heard some of the questions her aunt showered on her: Did they have to return the deposit? Would they be reimbursed for the food they'd already prepared for the event? The flowers? The decorations?

Melody narrowed her gaze toward Prince William. He stood on the railing talking to a woman about the same age as her aunts but kept glancing in Melody's direction as though he was surprised she hadn't taken her boxes and suitcase and left the dock.

Melody held his gaze as she answered her aunt's most repeated questions. "I have no idea why we were fired or if Prince Scrooge will reimburse us, and I intend to find out."

Melody handed the umbrella to her aunt and half-jogged, half-ran until she reached the yacht's ramp. Taking a deep breath, she swiped hair from her face and marched up the ramp to confront the Prince. Melody knew he'd noticed her. The muscles on his jaw tightened. Even so, he continued his conversation with the woman as though Melody were invisible, discussing something about weather conditions and when they expected a float plan to arrive.

Melody cleared her throat and prepared for battle. "May I speak with you a moment, Prince William?"

The muscles around his jaw tightened as he turned his storm-grey eyes in her direction. "No."

The word went off like a giant flare in her head. She clenched her hands at her sides, straightening to her full height of five feet eleven. "Unacceptable."

"I beg your pardon?" Again, that lift of an eyebrow, accompanied by a scowl, as though this were the Dark Ages and he was being forced to talk with a peasant or step over cow dung.

She jutted her jaw, crossed her arms, and tapped her foot. Well, her family might not be descended from royalty, but if her aunties' stories were even half true, Melody was descended from rebellious stock who never took no as an answer. "I'm not going anywhere until you answer my questions."

He whispered something to the woman, and she nodded and headed back inside. His superior look stayed frozen in place, except around the corners of his mouth. "You have my full attention."

Had Melody seen a ghost of a smile cross his features?

She shook away the silly notion and hardened her resolve. "You fired us, and my aunt and I deserve to know why." His unwavering glare unnerved her as another possible reason for the firing occurred to her. His father wasn't a young man. Was it possible that he had taken ill? Melody held her hand to her mouth. "Oh, no. Is your father sick? I'm so sorry. I…"

"My father is in good health."

She let out her breath. "That is incredibly good to hear. Did he or his bride-to-be change their mind?" Melody sighed. Romance may never have worked for her, but she loved knowing that it could happen for others. "Well, people changing their minds right before a wedding, that is not unheard of unfortunately, but if you read our contract, we require reimbursement for costs incurred. Would you like an itemized list?"

"My father didn't change his mind."

The words hung in the air as the woman the Prince had been talking with earlier reappeared. Melody's first impression of her was correct. She was about the age of Melody's aunts, but unlike them, she wore her salt and pepper hair short and was dressed conservatively in a dark blue suit and matching vest the shade of her eyes.

"Begging your pardon, Your Highness," the woman said, "but your guest has arrived: the Contessa Carlotta."

Prince William's eyebrows knitted together. "What about my father and his fiancée and the other guests?" He heaved a sigh. "Never mind. They might be arriving later. Thank you, Sydney." He turned back to Melody. "I will see that you are reimbursed for any expenses you incurred. If you will excuse me, I must find out what happened to delay my father and prepare to meet my guest."

And just like that Melody had been dismissed.

She stood alone on the deck, fighting the impulse to chase after the Prince.

And do what? He'd already agreed to reimburse them for any expenses. She should be pleased. This meant she didn't have to help her aunt create a wedding for rich people and could return to work and her sad little apartment.

Waves lapped against the sides of the yacht like white icing as Melody retraced her path down the steps to the dock. But it wasn't just that he would reimburse them; they would lose the sizable commission when the event was over. What about that money? Would he also make up for that loss?

More importantly, why had he rubbed her nerves so raw?

She paused on the dock, faced the yacht, and lifted her fist. "This is not over."

Chapter Six

The wind had died down with only a gentle breeze as a reminder of its fury. William stared after the wedding planner. He'd heard her shout that this wasn't over, and her voice had drawn him back outside. What had she meant? He'd offered to reimburse them.

She was talking with an older woman he suspected was one of her aunts. Melody had defied him. And despite all logic to the contrary he was intrigued. But it was not only her defiance that had taken him by surprise. It was her concern for his father. William had read the emotions on her lovely face. Her emotions had been clear and reflected in the shade of her eyes, the turn of her mouth, and the way she tilted her head.

There was no pretense about her. She was all business one moment as she positioned her lush lips in a straight line and tilted her head to meet his gaze. Then her mouth had softened, and her brown eyes had deepened to the color of maple syrup over concern for his father's health. And when she realized that his father still wanted to go forward with the wedding, her eyes had widened in defiance with specks of amber light. She was magnificent. If possible, she was even more attractive when she defied him. He had been caught in those eyes, lost in their depths, and left wondering what it would be like if those eyes turned toward him in passion.

"If you don't mind my saying, Your Highness, the meeting between you and the wedding planner didn't go very well."

William jolted out of his thoughts. Sydney, like Officer Perdy, had been with his family since before he was born and both were close to his father's age. Sydney always dressed formally in dark suits and rarely smiled, but she was kind and thoughtful and had been like a mother to him when his own mother had died.

He shook his head. "No, Sydney, it did not go well at all."

"She is rather attractive for an American."

"She's rather attractive for any woman." William's gaze lingered on Melody's hips as she swung away from the dock in the direction of her suitcase and the mountain of boxes. "What are you suggesting?"

Sydney shrugged. "Just an observation." She hesitated. "What will you tell your father when you announce that you turned the wedding planner away? It will not go down well."

"No, it will not."

Sydney was correct. His father would not take kindly to his son's interference. He watched Melody as she collapsed the umbrella he had given her and dumped it into a trash receptacle.

The corners of his mouth turned in a smile. He would find another way to delay, and with hope stop, his father from remarrying until William at least knew more about his father's fiancée. William had little doubt that Melody would contact his father and then there would be hell to pay.

"I've changed my mind. The wedding reception plans will go forward as scheduled."

"I presume the wedding planner and her party will accompany us to Victoria B.C.?"

"It would seem so."

"Does that also mean that you have abandoned your goal to dissuade your father from remarrying?"

William scrubbed his face with his hand. "Not in the least. But I have to play it smart."

The wedding planner stood near boxes that towered over her like cardboard soldiers, waiting for their orders. The morning sun peeked out of the clouds to touch her hair and turn it an autumn red. She reminded him of a general summoning her troops as she talked to the older woman and pointed at his yacht. She would not give up. For some reason that pleased him more than he wanted to admit.

"Your Highness…"

William tore his gaze from the dock. "The wedding planner needs help loading her boxes on board. Can you see to it? Melody McBride was correct. My father should be the person who cancels."

Sydney nodded again with a hint of a smile. "And what stateroom would you like me to assign to the wedding planner?"

William's first impulse was to ask that she stay in the stateroom closest to his. He turned his back to the dock and the musical laughter he knew belonged to Melody. It was a song that you couldn't quite place, conjuring a pleasant memory and holding your attention until the end. He fought the impulse to turn around. She had found humor in the situation instead of dwelling on the negative.

God help him. He had just met her and yet every fiber of his being was tuned into her: the way she walked, the way she laughed, and the way the sun danced over the amber highlights in her red hair.

Sydney stood as silent as a guard at Buckingham Palace, as though trying to read his mind. If she had, he doubted she would have gathered any useful information and would have believed him as daft as a bat. It was not like him to fall this hard this fast. He blamed lack of sleep, news regarding the cattle herd, and worry over his father's marriage announcement.

William headed in the direction of the galley for a strong cup of coffee to jolt him back to reality. "Please show the wedding planner to a stateroom that is as far away from my quarters as is logistically possible."

Chapter Seven

Melody laughed again as she scooped Charmer from the dock and into her arms, offering him a kitty treat in exchange for her house keys. Charmer had found Melody's keys and played a game of hide and seek until Melody had cornered him against the cardboard boxes of wedding decorations. "Settle down, you little scamp."

She settled Charmer in his cat carrier, latched the door, and gazed over at the *Royal Escape*. The Prince and the woman he had been talking to had gone inside, and the only activity was about a half dozen crew members working to secure the yacht. What was wrong with her? She'd yelled at the client. Well, he wasn't the client, exactly, but he was the client's son, and she hadn't yelled as much as talked very loudly and firmly.

This wasn't like her. She usually did the nod-and-smile thing and went along to get along, as her mother used to say. But something in her changed when she met the Prince, as though a light switch had been flipped. The infuriating man pushed every button, and some she hadn't known she possessed. One minute he was Prince Charming, and the next Mr. Scrooge (Prince of Darkness?). She eyed the umbrella she'd stuffed in the trash and narrowed her gaze. She should throw it in the water.

Aunty Cassy knelt to shove a few kitty-treats between the slats in the door. "I don't know what got into him."

"I agree. He had the nerve to cancel his father's wedding after all your hard work. I pushed back and he offered to at least reimburse us."

Aunty Cassy scrunched her eyebrows together. "I was talking about Charmer." She reached for Charmer's carrier and nodded in the direction of the yacht. "Why are those men from the yacht headed in our direction?"

The crew members wore matching black rain jackets and slacks with the woman the Prince had called Sydney leading the way.

Sydney came to a halt and surveyed the boxes and suitcases, then addressed Melody. "You made quite an impression on the Prince."

Melody groaned, remembering her claim that this wasn't over. "Please tell the Prince that I apologize."

Sydney winked. "I will do no such thing. Prince William has changed his mind regarding the wedding and reception and ordered that the crew and I escort you and your aunt on board."

Aunty Cassy clapped her hands. "That is wonderful news. If you don't mind my asking, is the Prince in the habit of changing his mind?"

Sydney directed the crew members to start carrying the boxes to the yacht. "Until now, the Prince has never changed his course once it was set. This was a first."

Chapter Eight

The crewmen Prince William had sent had carried Melody and her aunt's luggage and the wedding supplies to the yacht and deposited them in an enormous room that looked like it hadn't been updated since the nineteen-fifties. There was a musty smell: a mixture of old fabric, dust, and neglect. Tapered furniture legs and geometric patterns gave the room the futuristic feel so popular during that era. Her imagination itched to transform the room from tired and dated to retro chic. But had her aunts seen this place before they booked the event? Had they brought enough decorations to cover the flaws?

This wasn't Melody's first time on a yacht, but it would be the first time one left the dock with her on board. She was excited and a little bit nervous.

Her father had worked for a variety of boat dealers up and down the West Coast. She and her mother had worked countless boat shows, helping stage and decorate boats her father hoped to sell for the dealers. There was a vagabond aspect to that life that appealed to Melody. She loved traveling from place to place, but most of all, she loved transforming boring boat interiors into showstoppers. That life had changed when her parents had died.

Aunty Cassy set the cat carrier on the floor beside Melody. "This room is in desperate need of a Christmas tree."

Melody smiled and gave her aunt a hug. She knew her aunt loved the season of Christmas and its spirit of love and giving and believed it should be celebrated year-round. The summer after Melody's parents had died, Melody had been having a particularly bad day at school and came home to a house decorated like the inside of Santa's workshop. Her mood lifted that day and although her parents were gone, she realized she was not alone. Her aunts were her family.

As she drew back from her aunt's embrace, an idea sparked. "Your Christmas tree comment gave me a wonderful idea. What if we bring in more trees, decorate them with white lights, and create a wonderland-style setting for the rehearsal dinner and wedding?"

Aunty Cassy bent to release Charmer from his carrier. "Splendid idea. I'll make a few calls. We have time. The rehearsal dinner is not until tomorrow night."

"Your staterooms are ready," Sydney announced.

After watching the television series Downton Abbey, Sydney didn't fit Melody's impression of a person who worked for nobility. Instead of a formal and stiff expression, Sydney's smile was friendly and warm.

Charmer padded toward Sydney as though they were longtime friends. He lifted his head, inviting Sydney to pet him. Sydney obliged with a chuckle. "What a sweet kitty."

Aunty Cassy picked up the cat carrier. "He can be. This is a large yacht. How far away are the staterooms?"

Sydney gave Charmer a final gentle pat and straightened. "I took the liberty of placing each of you where I thought would best fit your needs. Cassy, as per your request, your stateroom is not far from here. Melody, your stateroom is a bit farther away, but one of our best cabins. I hope you don't mind the walk?"

"Not at all. In fact, I love to walk. If you had a hiking wall onboard that would be perfect."

Sydney's smile curled up at the edges. "We don't now, but you could ask Prince William. He is quite the outdoorsman and has an impressive gym onboard. His love of exercise is also why he choose the stateroom farthest from here. Come to think of it, his stateroom is near yours."

Charmer let out a low howl and scampered outside in the direction of the upper deck on the yacht.

"Now what?" Cassy said. "Melody, you have to go after him. No telling what he has in mind."

Melody smiled at her aunt's remark. Sometimes the aunts talked about Charmer as though he were a real person with human emotions and reactions. "Sydney, if you'll excuse me, I'll be right back. I'm sure Charmer just spotted a seagull, but no worries, I'll make sure he doesn't get into any mischief."

Her aunt mumbled something under her breath as Melody followed the direction Charmer had taken. The late afternoon sun was drifting low over the horizon as she climbed the stairs to the deserted upper deck. The area was large enough to hold a party of fifty guests comfortably. There were teak wood floors and built-in sofas, lounge chairs, and tables, all in a deep navy blue that looked almost black in the fading light.

She called for Charmer but only the breeze rustling through the ship's flags answered. To her knowledge, the cat had never been on a boat before. Melody raised her voice an octave higher. "Charmer. Where are you? This is not funny."

She heard a stressed howl followed by a weak meow and rushed toward the sound. Charmer perched on a ledge that spread out over the water. Even from a distance she could tell that the cat was shivering in fear. "Don't move," she shouted. "I'm coming."

A shadow moved near Charmer and took form. Prince William was balanced on the ledge and leaning toward the cat, whispering. The Prince held out his hand and paused, as though time weren't an issue.

Melody looked toward the sky. The wind and clouds were moving in again, and if there were a lightning strike, it might startle Charmer enough that the cat could lose his balance and fall into the freezing water. Melody edged closer slowly so as not to spook either the Prince or Charmer.

The Prince had moved closer to Charmer as well and continued to whisper in soothing tones. Suddenly, the Prince reached for Charmer, cradled the cat securely in his arms, and jumped from the ledge to the deck.

Melody let out a relieved breath and rushed over. "You saved him."

The Prince chuckled as he handed Charmer into Melody's arms. "I am sure your cat wasn't in any real danger. I was on the bridge and saw him chase after a seagull. He probably did not need my help, but with this crazy weather I did not want to take any chances. Besides, cats do not like water, so I'm sure he would not have jumped in after the seagull."

Melody cradled Charmer close as he purred. "Don't be so sure. Charmer isn't like most cats. He has been known to jump into the water and pretend he can't swim on more than one occasion. It's sort of his thing."

"Why would he do such a thing?"

"Well, my aunts used to be matchmakers before they retired."

"What does that have to do with your cat loving the water?"

Melody opened her mouth to explain, then snapped it shut. There was no way she could offer an explanation that would sound rational. Charmer had the habit of putting himself in harm's way at the exact moment when a couple her aunts were trying to match appeared on the scene. Her aunts called Charmer their secret weapon in the war of love. The most recent example was with Elizabeth and Eric last summer when Charmer had fallen into the water at the Kirkland Marina allegedly needing to be rescued.

No, there was no way to explain Charmer's behavior that would make sense.

"I should take Charmer back inside," Melody said. "Thank you for your help."

"My pleasure."

Melody turned to go and then cast another look in the Prince's direction. He smiled in return and she felt a glow of warmth spread over her face. The man was confusing. One minute he was true to his royal pedigree, behaving arrogantly, and the next he'd gone out on a literal ledge to rescue Charmer.

She tore her gaze from his and retraced her steps to the main room on the yacht where she'd left her aunt. Charmer purred in her arms, all innocent and cuddly. "I know what you're trying to do, and it won't work. I'm not in the least interested in Prince William."

Chapter Nine

William took a deep breath as he knocked on the stateroom he had assigned to the Contessa Carlotta. He could not, as much as he tried, banish Melody from his mind. She was stubborn, outspoken, and the most intriguing woman he had ever met. And cute. God help him. She was so adorable.

When he had seen the cat trot out on the ledge, he raced forward not realizing it belonged to Melody and her aunt. He was grateful for the impulse, though. The gratitude that shone in Melody's eyes when he handed over Charmer had been worth his yacht's weight in gold. For a moment their gaze had locked, and he saw a bright future in her eyes.

He shook free of the image of kisses under mistletoe, toasting the New Year, planning a life together… "Stop."

Once they landed in Victoria, they would never see each other again.

He ignored the knot in his throat that formed with that realization and knocked on Carlotta's door again, concentrating on the current problem. William did not understand why Carlotta was the only one who had arrived. He had expected an entourage comprised of his father's fiancée's family, as well as two of his father's lifetime friends. Instead, Carlotta had arrived alone. He had tried phoning his father, but the call had gone straight to voicemail.

William knocked a third time and heard Carlotta's muffled reply to enter.

The cabin had been designed and built to his grandfather's specifications when the yacht was under construction. His grandfather's favorite color had been purple, and entering the room was like falling into a vat of crushed grapes. It was the most spacious room on the yacht, with a separate bedroom, large sitting area with a fully stocked bar, walk-in closets, and a balcony. This was where his grandfather had stayed when he had hosted parties that had become legendary for all the wrong reasons. William never used it himself, saving it for when his father visited.

But when he entered, Carlotta was not alone. Perdy set a tray of sliced fruit and an assortment of cheese on the table and gave a slight bow. "Will that be all, Contessa?"

She lounged on the sofa and reached for a strawberry. "Perhaps later you can bring me a bottle of champagne with two glasses."

He bowed again, gave a nod to William, and exited the cabin with a smile on his face. Perdy had shaved, changed into his dress uniform, and looked in a good mood. Of the three, the last was the most puzzling. Perdy was never in a good mood.

William stared after Perdy until the man had closed the door, vowing to question the man later. But then he dismissed the idea as he walked over and opened the drapes to let in the gentler, softer rays of the afternoon sun to help neutralize the purple. It didn't help. Being in a good mood, no matter how unusual, wasn't cause for concern.

"Did Perdy provide you with everything you needed?"

"Almost," Carlotta said, her voice like a purr. She finished the strawberry and wiped her fingers on a linen napkin. She reclined on a sofa of ribbon taffeta and patted the space beside her, indicating William sit beside her.

Carlotta's blond-white hair was pulled back in a ponytail, and she wore a light cream-colored pantsuit trimmed in pale violet. She was dressed to complement the room, a trait he had learned about her on her visit to New Zealand.

He declined the offer, too on edge to sit still. "Do you know why my father did not arrive with you?"

She tossed a whisp of hair off her forehead and laughed. "Always direct. A quality you inherited from your father. He chartered a plane, and he and the wedding party went directly to Victoria B.C. After the long flight from Europe, the thought of boarding another plane, when I could luxuriate on your yacht, was an easy choice to make. So here I am."

His plans to have a private talk with his father concerning his sudden marriage announcement were slipping away. This was a disaster. "What about the rehearsal dinner and the marriage ceremony?" He heard the desperate edge to his voice but pushed forward. "There is a wedding planner onboard, who I'm assuming plans to transform this boat into some romancy, fairytale wonderland that will have my crew threatening to mutiny. Does my father wish to cancel?"

There was a knock on the door followed by Perdy's announcement that he'd brought the champagne.

"Just in time," Carlotta said in a rush. "Come in, Perdy." As Perdy entered and prepared to open the bottle, Carlotta continued. "Your father was insistent that the wedding planner and her people continue decorating and proceed with us to Victoria B.C. He said everything will go on as planned; there were just a few minor adjustments."

Perdy popped the champagne cork and filled two crystal glasses. Instead of the traditional gold shade, the champagne was rose-pink and reminded William of the wedding planner's lips and the glow of her face.

William rubbed the back of his neck, trying to ease the tension in his shoulders. The best thing to do was to stay busy. He would reach out to his ranch manager in New Zealand for progress on the investigation of the sick cattle, send word to the wedding planner and tell her that the rehearsal dinner was postponed until they reached their destination, chart their course for tomorrow's voyage, and avoid the wedding planner at all costs. He did not have time for a relationship. Every one he had been in had crashed and burned. The women he dated were more interested in the prospect of becoming a princess than of building a life with him.

It felt different with the wedding planner. She had not been impressed when she had learned he was a prince. In fact, her reaction had been the direct opposite, which had amused him in a good way.

But what was wrong with him? No woman had ever affected him the way she had. Was it just that she hadn't been impressed that he was a prince, or something more? He needed to clear his head. After he completed his list of tasks what he needed was a long workout in the yacht's gym.

"I apologize, Carlotta. I'm not in the mood for champagne."

Chapter Ten

Melody glanced at the stateroom key Sydney had given her as she pulled her suitcase down the yacht's long corridor, lined on either side with framed black and white drawings of sailing ships. According to Sydney, Melody's room was at the end of the hall. She was relieved for the break; she hadn't realized how on edge she felt until she'd left the main room of the ship. She kept thinking that at any moment the Prince would show up, and his presence was confusing and not something she wanted to examine too closely.

It had taken Melody longer than expected to help her aunt inventory the decoration boxes in the main room and leave messages to their vendors that they needed trees delivered before they sailed in the morning. It was worrisome their vendors hadn't returned their calls, but it was almost Christmas.

She could tell her aunt was tired, so Melody had suggested they go to their rooms, have meals delivered, and check back with each other in a few hours after they'd eaten. The good news was that the rehearsal dinner wasn't until tomorrow night, so she and her aunt had tonight and all day tomorrow to prepare.

The number of the room at the end of the hall matched her key and she unlocked the door and entered. Then stopped dead in her tracks.

Melody stood in the middle of her stateroom and turned around in a circle as though she had stepped into a dream. Picture windows framed Lake Union harbor and the boats moored nearby. In the center of the room was a king size bed with an anchor-patterned comforter, flanked by honey-colored teak cabinets. There was also a separate sitting area with a table graced by a shell-shaped bowl filled with fresh fruit and cheese. The walls were covered with full-sized photos of sea life, and several closed doors, which she guessed led to a bathroom or other rooms.

The crisp, blue, green, and white room had a restful feel and worked its magic to ease her jumbled thoughts. She dropped the room key on the table along with her purse and left her suitcase, meandering over to the window to enjoy the last golden rays of the winter sun as it disappeared over the horizon. Waves lapped against the sides of the yacht and the tension in her neck eased.

Melody glanced toward one of the closed doors, which she guessed led to the bathroom. She'd bet the bathroom housed a large soaking tub with a big picture window. There might even be candles and fluffy towels. She fished for her cellphone and calculated whether she'd have time before she met with her aunt.

Her decision made she headed toward the door, turned the knob, and entered. She'd guessed right. The bathroom was enormous and seemed to go on forever. It carried the same nautical feel as the main cabin and was floor-to-ceiling white marble, shot through with slate grey and decorated with sea life accessories. There was a large soaking tub on her right with a window with drawn curtains that faced the harbor and a corridor to her left that led to a glass shower.

She sighed in delight and slipped off her shoes and sweater. The only thing missing was candles.

The shower turned on. It must have turned on by itself.

She headed over to turn it off and ran straight into a naked Prince William.

His body was hard, and his muscles flexed under her touch as she clung to his shoulders to keep her balance. Her body jolted on fire as she shoved against him to distance herself. She turned away to hide what she knew was a flame red blush. The man was built like a body builder: broad shoulders, rock hard abs, narrow waist… She slammed her eyes shut. She'd seen everything.

Her voice shook. "What are you doing here?"

"Me? You are in my bathroom."

"Your bathroom?" She snapped back toward him. "But Sydney gave me a key to this…" She froze. He was still naked. She shut her eyes and turned away again. "I'll leave. Sydney must have given me the wrong key."

Melody snagged her shoes and sweater and ran out of the bathroom as though she were being chased by a swarm of bees and headed for her suitcase. She pulled her sweater over her head and slipped on her shoes at the same time. It wasn't that she hadn't seen a naked man before, but what a man. Her face still felt like she had stood too close to a blazing fire.

"Wait."

His voice, deep and too sexy, stopped her in her tracks. She didn't turn. She kept her eyes averted and concentrated on slipping her purse over her shoulder and fishing the key from the bowl on the table. "I apologize. I must have read the number on the room wrong."

He reached around her and took the key from her hand, his fingers brushing against hers. His casual touch sparked through her, flaming her face. Don't look, the Puritan side of her lectured. But her rebellious side won the battle.

Melody slid her gaze toward him. He wasn't naked but close. He'd draped a towel around his waist and for some reason that was sexier. She visualized slipping her hand between his waist and the towel as she gently pulled it down. Maybe he leaned toward her.

She cleared her throat. "I should leave."

"Don't." His smile was boyish and stopped her heart. "I mean. I want you to stay."

Every nerve in her body shouted yes, and she mentally visualized what his skin would taste like if it were slathered with whipped cream. She wrenched out of the fantasy and ordered her lusty thoughts to take a cold shower.

"I can't. We just met." Her inner goddess screamed coward. She pressed her lips together and laughed nervously. "That came out wrong. I know you didn't mean that we stay here together."

His smile sobered and he returned the key to her hand. "Sydney must have given you the key to my stateroom by mistake. You can keep the room. I will move to the cabin across the hall." He paused and moved aside as though to free a path to the door. "And for the record, and as crazy as it seems, I wanted you to spend the night with me."

Chapter Eleven

The next day was overcast and gray, reflecting William's mood. Last night, after his inappropriate comment to Melody that they spend the evening together, he'd given her his stateroom and chosen one closer to the bridge. Had he really told Melody that he wanted to sleep with her?

He groaned. He was losing it. He did not know what it was about her that made him want to tell her how he felt as though he might lose the opportunity if he didn't.

William had called Perdy this morning to let him know he was on his way, but Perdy had told him not to hurry. Willian could have sworn he heard a woman's laugher in the background but dismissed it as background noise. William debated whether to confront Sydney regarding the mix-up with stateroom keys. It was not like her to give a guest the wrong key, especially one that belonged to the Prince's private stateroom. He remembered Melody's reaction to him and grinned. He should give Sydney a raise.

As he neared the main room on the yacht, he heard a scream coming from that direction. He raced toward the sound, and in a matter of minutes entered the room. The cat, Charmer, screamed again as it leapt into an empty box, only to be pulled out and scolded by Melody.

The cat's protests weren't the only issue. Boxes were ripped open, and decorations scattered over the floor in wild abandon. Melody sat on the floor near an overstuffed chair, digging into the contents of a box like a pirate searching for treasure.

William stepped over plastic pumpkins, bouquets of fake orange and yellow flowers, as well as New Year's Eve and Valentine decorations until he reached Melody. "Can I help?" He was not sure exactly how he could help, but it seemed the right thing to say.

She startled slightly, her face turning a blush pink as she averted her gaze. "Only if you can change these decorations into Santa Clauses and poinsettia plants."

He knelt beside her and picked out a straw scarecrow with a black bird on its shoulder. "That's beyond my abilities, I'm afraid."

"Aunty Cassy's too."

"I beg your pardon?"

She shook her head. "Never mind. Well, we're going to have to figure something out. My aunts promised your father and his fiancée a Christmas themed rehearsal dinner and wedding. I tried to call our vendors again, but no one is picking up. If we just had more trees, we could at least decorate them with lights."

He liked that she included him. "Trees are my specialty. I will make a few calls."

Melody leaned against a sofa as Charmer padded over and curled up on her lap. "Thank you, but what are we going to tell your father? He's going to take one look at the Halloween, Valentine, and New Year's Eve decorations, know we messed up, and fire us on the spot."

"He is not going to fire you."

"How can you be so sure? A short time ago you wanted to fire my aunt and me."

He reached over and scratched Charmer behind his ear. "I had my reasons but as it turns out, my father and his fiancée never arrived. He called and said they had a change in plans and would meet us in Victoria."

She paused, turning toward him with a question in her beautiful eyes. "Do you mind if I ask why you wanted to fire us in the first place?"

"It is…complicated."

"I'm told I'm a good listener. Sometimes it is easier to confess to a perfect stranger than a person we've known for a long time."

He looked over at the hodge podge of decorations scattered over the floor. Instead of an unsettled mess, the sight was soothing, like fall leaves on a forest floor. "You do not seem like a stranger to me." He let his comment linger like a warm breeze.

Charmer leapt up and scampered over to the boxes to investigate a plastic pumpkin with a happy face painted in black glitter.

Melody drew her legs against her chest. She stared at Charmer as he moved from the pumpkin to investigate a roll of orange ribbon.

He changed the subject and didn't answer her.

"I feel the same way about you," Melody said. "Why do you suppose that is?" She slid her gaze toward his. "It feels like we are friends already. Do you believe there is such a thing as an instant connection?"

"I didn't until now. You have enchanted me body and soul."

Chapter Twelve

A few hours later, Melody leaned on the railing as the midday sun peeked from behind the clouds. She pulled her autumn-gold wool shawl around her shoulders, thinking she should have worn her coat instead. The air was crisp and cold with the promise of snow. She could go inside for something warmer to wear, but she didn't want to leave her vantage point. Prince William mentioned his father and fiancée planned to meet the yacht when it docked in Victoria Harbor.

Her aunts hadn't given her much in the way of a description of the couple, and the only thing she knew was that they were sweethearts at a university in London and had reconnected recently after the deaths of their spouses. The story had sounded so romantic and the second chance aspect was what Melody knew had hooked her aunts into helping the couple plan a destination wedding.

Seagulls floated overhead, and the faint sound of bagpipes drifted toward her from the harbor. She loved the approach to

Victoria. It had been her parents' favorite vacation spot and held warm memories.

The yacht slowed down once it reached the outer harbor and eased into Victoria, gliding with care past tour boats and smaller ships, so as not to create too much wake and accidentally swamp the vessels. It reminded Melody of how she envisioned parents might enter the room on Christmas morning, while their children rushed to find their presents under the tree.

Year-round, Victoria drew people to its shores, but Christmas time was magical, and the Empress hotel was the star on the top of the tree.

"It is hard to look away."

She nodded, recognizing Prince William's voice.

"Please stay right there. I have something for you."

She smiled as he turned and disappeared into the main cabin. The tone of his voice was like warm caramel drizzled over a dark chocolate cookie laced with cinnamon and nutmeg. Just like a dessert, his voice had layers of emotion and texture she wanted to explore. When she'd first met him, his voice had been as hard and impenetrable as steel and yet there had been something about him, a hidden depth that promised more.

Last night and this morning that promise had been fulfilled, and his voice had been playful. Today it held something else again. The playfulness had turned flirtatious.

She shouldn't like him. She had told her aunts over and over that she didn't believe in instant attraction. And, of course, he was not her type. He didn't possess any of the qualities on the list she'd developed her freshman year in college. She wanted a man who loved hiking and the out of doors, wanted a home and family, and loved animals. The articles her aunt had given her regarding the Prince described him as a corporate lawyer and a recluse who did little else than manage his family's holdings in New Zealand. There was a hint that he had been engaged but not how it had ended.

And then there was the issue that he was a prince, with all the baggage that she heard went along with royalty and the uber rich. Examples of those types engaged in wild parties littered the internet, highlighting their faults. They were self-centered, lazy, entitled, lacked empathy, and never thought of anyone but themselves.

Prince William reemerged holding a cup of steaming hot chocolate in each hand. "I thought you might like hot cocoa."

She warmed under his gaze.

Okay, so maybe this particular prince was at least thoughtful.

She accepted the hot cocoa and blew to cool it down. Steam rose and laced the air with the fragrance of yummy chocolate. "Thank you." She took a sip. "When do we meet your father and his fiancée?"

He stared at his cup. "They were to meet us at the Empress Hotel for high tea, but there has been another change of plans."

She took another sip, hearing a change in the tone of his voice. He was clearly upset. "Is anything wrong?"

He took a deep swallow of the hot chocolate and turned his head in the direction of a float plane as it made its approach. "I wish I knew. Father called when I went in for the cocoa."

Melody reached out and put her hand on his arm as her pulse quickened. Since she was a child, she dreaded hearing people cancel. In her experience, it meant illness or worse. "Are your father and his fiancée all right?"

He rested his free hand on hers and smiled. "Yes, my father sounded fine and actually we had a good conversation. I am sure it is nothing. Although he has been this way since reconnecting with Deloris. He was never the spontaneous type. In that regard he and I are very alike. I plan out everything and take a long time to decide." He took a drink and continued to focus on the harbor. "That is honest. I tried to convince my father to have his fiancée sign a prenuptial agreement. It didn't go very well."

A cool breeze swept over the harbor, teasing the water into white caps as it ruffled Melody's hair and tugged her shawl from her grasp. Her shawl floated into the air, then flew over the water as though it had sprouted wings.

Prince William set his hot chocolate on the deck, removed his jacket, and spread it over her shoulders, pulling her close. He buttoned his jacket around her as a muscle twisted on his jaw. "I'm struggling. I don't want my father to get hurt."

She heard the pain and the love in his voice and the vulnerability. On an impulse, she rose on tiptoes and kissed him on the lips. "You will be there for your father regardless of the outcome. That is the strength of belonging to a family. My aunts have a saying: Love is worth the leap of faith."

Chapter Thirteen

Melody couldn't stop smiling as she chose a sweater from a selection that her aunt had spread over the beds and every available space in the cabin. She had to hurry. She had told William she would meet him on deck within the hour to view the Christmas Ship parade.

"You must have cleaned out a store of all their available Christmas-themed sweaters," Melody said. "There is every style and size imaginable."

Her aunt moved a sweater from a chair, tossed it on a table, and sat. "I believe in being prepared. You never know who might feel the Christmas spirit."

"And nothing says Christmas spirit like a sweater with a reindeer outlined in gold sequins."

Aunty Cassy stuck out her tongue at her niece. "You are making fun, but you have to admit there is something wonderfully silly and child-like about wearing a sweater like the one you describe."

Melody laughed softly. "You have a point." She held up a Christmas poinsettia sweater and discarded it for one with snowmen, then changed her mind and selected a sweater decorated with a Christmas tree outlined in green sequins, with bells where the ornaments would have been. "The limo for Butchart Gardens leaves in ten minutes; aren't you coming? The Prince's father is meeting us there with his fiancée."

Aunty Cassy peered over a new set of reading glasses dusted with green glitter. She reached for a patchwork quilted lap blanket and settled back in her chair. "I plan to have an early night. Tomorrow will be a busy day. Besides, I have met the sweet couple and you need to spend more time with your prince."

Melody grabbed a red hat that matched the sweater. "Prince William is not *my* prince. We just met and are barely friends."

"You know my opinion on that subject. Time has nothing to do with a connection to a person's soulmate. Sometimes it can take decades to recognize the spark of attraction, as in the case of the Prince's father and his fiancée. Other times it only takes a first meeting, as in the example of you and…"

"Do not go there," Melody said, reaching for her coat on the bed.

Her aunt shrugged. "Ignoring the attraction between you and the Prince won't make it go away."

Melody leaned over and gave her aunt a peck on the cheek. "You are incorrigible. Do you ever take a break from matchmaking?"

Her aunt patted her on the cheek. "Where would be the fun in that?"

Melody glanced at the clock on the cabin wall shaped like an anchor. "I'm late. Are you sure you will be okay here on your own?"

"Silly, child. I am not alone. The crew is remaining on board, and the cook promised to make me his famous fish stew for dinner tonight."

"That sounds suspiciously like a date. Early night, you say? I doubt that seriously. I know the real reason you are staying behind. I noticed the way you looked at the cook, and he toward you. I could almost see the sparks fly."

Her aunt straightened the blanket on her lap. "Pish, posh. Now who is the one playing matchmaker?"

Melody winked. "It must be in the blood. Have to go." She buttoned her coat, rushed out of her cabin, and straight into Prince William's arms. "Your Highness, I'm so sorry. I was in such a hurry. I didn't want to miss the bus to Butchart Gardens."

His smile was disarming. "I would like it very much if you called me William."

"William," she whispered, then cocked her head. "What about my calling you Will?"

He leaned closer. "Only when we are alone."

She loved the sound of that. She nodded, then narrowed her gaze. "What are you wearing? Your father asked us to wear something Christmasy?"

Will patted the holly boutonniere he had attached to his lapel. "I am honoring my father's request, and to be clear, what was said was to wear something that reflected the holiday season. What about you?"

She unbuttoned her coat and displayed her Christmas sweater. "Ta dah!"

Will frowned. "That is hideous."

She jumped up and down so that the bells on her sweater chimed. "It's Christmasy."

He put his hands on her shoulders as though to settle her down. "Why are you in such a good mood?"

"I don't have the slightest idea." She paused and her grin widened. "Yes, I do. I thought it would bother me that we were coming to Victoria in December. The last time I was here I was with my parents and it was our last Christmas together. Instead of feeling sad, however, all I can think about are the wonderful memories we shared. I am especially excited to see Butchart Gardens. My parents wanted to take me there, but the weather turned stormy and we decided not to go. They promised we'd go the following year..." Her voice trailed off as the weight of the pain returned.

Will lifted her chin and brushed a tear that had escaped her cheek. His voice was soft and warm and full of comfort. "That means you will be seeing the gardens during Christmas for the first time. A magical time. It was my mother's favorite place."

And like magic, the threatening cloud over her lifted. It wasn't his words, but the emotion they expressed. "Yes, for the first time," she whispered. "You mother visited Victoria?"

"Many times. She said it reminded her of England. She especially loved the gardens, not just in winter, but all year long."

"You must miss her."

"Every day."

"I miss my parents too."

The silence surrounded her, swirling around and around. A comfortable silence. He touched her face and her eyes brimmed. "Which means you need a sweater."

He narrowed his gaze. "I do not understand. How is your seeing the gardens at Christmas for the first time mean that I have to wear a hideous sweater?"

"Do I need a reason? And even if I agreed, there is no time to shop."

She reached for his hand and drew him into the cabin. "Then it's a good thing my aunt brought along a supply. By the way, do you like reindeers on your sweater or kittens?"

Chapter Fourteen

Melody leaned on the railing of the yacht as the day turned to night and a light sprinkling of snow began to fall. They could have departed for Victoria sooner, but the goal was to arrive in the Puget Sound as the Christmas ships were making their rounds around the water. She had seen the ships from the land side, but never on the water, and as soon as Will had learned that factoid, the decision to leave later had been decided.

Will spread a blanket around her shoulders as he moved beside her on the railing. "Are you sure you want to stay outside since it has started to snow? It will be warmer inside."

She glanced toward the main cabin. Everyone had moved inside and were pressed against the windows for the best view. She shook her head. "I like it right where we are. It feels like we are alone. Inside will be too crowded."

He pulled her against him and kissed her lightly. "My thoughts exactly. I will keep you warm."

"I never doubted it for a minute." She straightened. "Look over there. I think that is one of the Christmas ships making its way to the festival. Can you make the yacht go faster?"

He chuckled. "Yes, if we were on the open seas. No worries, we will see them all soon enough."

She snuggled against him. "Are you always so patient?"

"Not normally. Except right now I want time to slow down so I can savor every second with you."

"You have to stop doing that."

"I beg your pardon?"

"You always say the most romantic things."

"Why is that a bad thing? I am with the woman I love."

His words caught her off guard, although if she were honest, they did not come as a surprise. His admission had been building since they first met. "I love you too," she said on a whisper as she spread her arm over his waist and leaned against his chest.

He kissed her again and pointed to the ship she had mentioned earlier. "That ship has been outlined with lights to resemble Santa's sleigh and reindeer."

Melody pointed to another ship that was joining the parade. "And that one is covered with Christmas trees and snowmen. Did you know that the first Christmas ship festival started in nineteen forty-one?"

Will's arms tightened around her in a loving embrace. "When you come to New Zealand, we can start the tradition."

His comments seemed a natural progression of their relationship, and she welcomed the possibility and all that it represented. Tonight seemed like anything and everything was possible. Her aunts believed in love at first sight, and her parents were living proof that it could happen. So, why not for their daughter?

The parade grew as snow danced around her. Each ship was more elaborate than the last. Some had cartoon character themes, giant vintage trains, circus themes, or Ferris wheels, all outlined in lights, while others were decorated with fairytale story themes like Cinderella, Snow White and the Seven Dwarfs, or Sleeping Beauty. The creativity was endless.

And snuggled in Will's arms, she never wanted her time with him to end.

Chapter Fifteen

It was well past nine o'clock in the evening when *The Royal Escape* docked in Victoria Harbor, and Melody felt like time had passed like a magical dream. Their limo drove past the grounds of the Empress Hotel, which had been transformed into a Christmas wonderland. Lights outlined the massive Parliament Buildings, streetlights bordered walkways, and Christmas carolers strolled along wide sidewalks spreading holiday cheer. Vendors sold roasted chestnuts as well as Christmas wreaths and baskets of poinsettias. Melody understood why her parents loved this place. It had an old-fashioned, Charles Dickens' feel that warmed a person down to their toes.

The twelve to fourteen-mile limo drive from the harbor to Butchart Gardens was estimated to take a short twenty-five minutes. It seemed the trip would never end. At the last minute Carlotta had joined them, decked out in a thigh-high black-wool dress covered with silver crystals. She monopolized the conversation and alternated between grilling Melody on her likes and dislikes, ranging from dark versus light chocolate, work experience, and then leapt on Melody's interest in hiking and rock climbing. Melody thought she was in a job interview and was relieved when Carlotta switched her attention to William.

Melody learned that Will couldn't identify a rose from a dandelion, had never hunted and never had been interested, swam like a fish, and only walked along the beach if he had somewhere to go.

When Carlotta asked him about birds and land and marine animals in New Zealand the tone of his voice became more animated. He named all the birds from the albatross to the White Heron, mentioned that the only native animal was a bat or what the Māori people of New Zealand called pekapeka. When he talked about blue, humpback, and sperm whales he sounded like a boy talking about a new train set. Then he mentioned the orca or killer whale and reached for Melody's hand and said that he wanted to invite Melody to climb the MacKinnon Pass with him in New Zealand on the land where Lord of the Rings had been filmed.

Carlotta's questions ended when the limo pulled to a stop. Carlotta rolled down the window. "Look, we've arrived at Butchart Gardens."

The driver exited the limo and opened the door, a blast of the frigid air blowing inside. The sound of Carlotta's complaints rolled away as Will exited the limo and reached for Melody's hand.

Lights in blues, greens, reds, yellows, and silver lined the trees on either side of the walkway. Semi-transparent angel statues, glittering with silver and gold lights, beckoned guests toward the archway of lights formed in the shape of roses, pansies, daisies, lilacs, and hanging wisteria. Melody gasped at the beauty as Will drew her under the archway into a wonderland of lights. It was as though the terraced gardens had been painted with millions and millions of colored lights. Green border lights framed carpets of blue lights, then meandered to circle bright pink lights. Lights outlined statues of deer, rabbits, and nesting birds.

"It's breathtaking," Melody said.

"It is indeed. May I steal a kiss?"

With her nod, Will leaned down and kissed her gently. The kiss was feather soft and light as a warm breeze. The moment their lips touched a spark lit up her senses. She opened her eyes to meet Will's gaze. He had felt it as well.

"Wow," was all he said as he moved a breath away.

She smiled against his lips. "Wow!"

"I'm going on ahead," Carlotta said.

Will drew Melody's hand through the crook his arm and led her in the direction of a path lined with white lights. "My father mentioned when I talked to him this morning that once we left the parking lot, we should follow the path that leads to the waterfall. That is where we are headed."

The path led around trees dripping with glowing icicles and twinkling fairy lights. The gardens were infused with magic and possibilities.

She wound her other arm through his and leaned against him as they strolled over the path feeling bold. "Should we talk about the kiss?"

"It wasn't just a kiss."

She shook her head. "No, it wasn't. I don't believe in..."

"...love at first sight," he finished, leaning to kiss her on the head. "Neither did I. Until I met you. Was it only yesterday?"

She reached out to one of the fairy lights, watching the play of light on her fingers. "This is magical. Do you think this is real?"

"Are you talking about the lights or us?"

Us. She loved the sound of that word. She closed her eyes and drew in a deep breath. It felt as though she had known Will all her life. "I think I'm talking about both. This can't be happening."

"You mean the part where we shouldn't be attracted to each other to this degree after knowing each other for less than two days?"

"Has it only been two days?"

"It seems longer, doesn't it?"

She nodded. "A wonderful lifetime."

An archway rose over the path and was covered with real white roses intertwined with dripping fairy lights and sprinkled with red and green berry-shaped lights. Under the archway a couple appeared. The man, with his Sean Connery-style salt and pepper beard, wore a dark suit, and the woman a long-sleeved cream-colored suit. The woman had white hair trimmed below her chin in a fashionable bob. They both looked familiar.

"Welcome, son," said the older gentlemen as he held out his hand toward Will. He smiled toward Melody. "It is good to see you again so soon."

Christmas music floated on the air as lacy snowflakes danced in the night sky. Out of the corner of her eye, Melody noticed her aunts Isadora and Shawna take a seat beside Cassy. Melody glanced again at Will's father and his fiancée. "I met you outside my aunt's café."

DeDe tugged on Will's father's arm.

"We should go. They are ready for the ceremony to begin."

"How do you know my father?" asked Will.

Melody glanced over at Aunty Casey and received a knowing wink. Melody laughed softly, finally placing the couple that were about to marry. They admitted to meeting with her aunts to arrange a match for their son.

She squeezed Will's hand. "I'll fill you in, but it looks like my aunts aren't the only ones who believe in love at first sight."

Chapter Sixteen

William stood beside his father as DeDe walked down an aisle lit with thousands of lights to the sound of Christmas carolers who were dressed as though they had stepped out of a Charles Dickens' novel. DeDe carried a bouquet of white poinsettias and seemed like a woman who smiled often. Her smile broadened when she met his father Tom's adoring gaze. William had to admit that he had never seen his father more relaxed or happy.

Melody had filled him in on the part his father and DeDe had played in matchmaking. He was surprised it hadn't bothered him. The relationship with Melody was still in its early stages but he couldn't shake the feeling that it could build into something lasting and real.

When the vows were exchanged and his father and Deloris were pronounced married, William felt as though a weight had been lifted off his shoulders. They kissed and walked back down the aisle as husband and wife, while William searched for Melody.

She was at his side before he had a chance to draw another breath. She reached up and kissed him. "I love weddings. But don't tell my aunts."

"Your secret is safe with me." With those words he knew he meant even more. He knew he could trust her. But how? Why did he feel such a strong connection to Melody? He knew next to nothing about her, and yet, he felt like he had known her all his life. That reoccurring theme had played in his mind since the moment they first met. "Would you like to explore the gardens?"

"Don't we have to attend the reception at the restaurant?"

He glanced toward his father, and as though they could read each other's minds, his father turned and nodded with a smile, mouthing the word, "*Go*."

William reached for Melody's hand, basking in the glow of how natural it had become. He led her through an archway lit with lights shaped like holly berries and onto a path that circled in the direction of a carousel and ice rink. "Do you know how to ice skate?"

"No, why do you ask?"

"I can teach you."

"Or I could watch you skate."

"Where would be the fun in that?"

"For starters, there wouldn't be any falling involved."

He slowed at the entrance of the ice rink. Couples were skating together, holding hands, stealing a kiss, or ice dancing to the Christmas carolers. "You will not fall. I won't let you."

He drew her in an embrace. "I want an excuse to hold you in my arms."

She raised up on tiptoes and kissed him on the mouth lightly. "Well, why didn't you say so in the first place. Where do we rent the skates?"

...to be continued

Bio

Pam Binder is a USA Today and New York Times bestselling author who loves Irish and Scottish myths and legends. She is a conference speaker, president of the Pacific Northwest Writers Association, and teaches two year-long novel writing courses. In additional to writing stories about immortal highlanders, Pam writes the romance time travel series, The Matchmaker Café as well as the Young Adult Irish fantasy series, Goblin Bones. She also loves writing Christmas stories. *Christmas Knight* was published last year, and her newest contemporary, *Christmas Deadline*, was released, November, 2020.

A Canadian Christmas

Darcy Carson

Dedication

To my friend, Shellie Brandon. I've never known anyone
who loves Christmas more than you.

Chapter One

Amy Phillips peered out the window of the Via Rail train car and watched incredible scenery whizz past. Mostly tall, skinny pole pines that reminded her of giant toothpicks, and towering mountains of the Canadian Rockies with snow-covered sides that emphasized jagged edges. Patches of snow clung to tree branches and blanketed the ground. She'd always loved snow. Winter was her favorite time of the year.

After landing the biggest deal of her real estate career, it meant she could treat herself to a luxury vacation. She had booked a few days at the Banff Fairmont Hotel to celebrate her success. Christmas in Canada.

She hadn't taken a vacation in…

Pausing to scratch her head, she wracked her mind. How long? The answer refused to come. Was she brain dead? Or was it because she hated admitting the truth? It had only been a couple years, not more than five.

Liar…try ten years.

No way. That couldn't be right. Could it? Where had time flown? Yet, deep down Amy knew the root cause. Her career came first.

The hum of rails was interrupted when the first call to dinner came over the intercom. Two women—one long-legged in caramel-colored pants and top with a paisley shawl wrapped around broad shoulders and light brown hair that contained matching highlights to her outfit, and the other wearing a blue pants suit, with her hair a web of silver—hustled past her deep in conversation. She followed in their wake, all three rocking side-to-side with the train's jarring movement. At the first door, the younger woman yanked it wide and sped through without waiting for the second woman.

How rude.

Amy hurried forward where the well-rounded woman struggled to open it. Up close, she caught the faint smell of lavender perfume. "Here, let me hold that for you. It looks heavy." She turned to see wrinkles covering the woman's face, but the lines added character and made her look sweet.

For a moment the woman stood, her grey eyebrows knitting in contemplation. "Thank you, honey."

Amy pulled the door into the connecting space between cars, felt the bite of mountain chill, before pushing the next door, always making sure the older woman was free and clear. She did this at each coupling until reaching the dining car.

The hostess rushed forward. "Mrs. Townsend, welcome. Welcome. Your table is ready for you. I hope you enjoy your meal."

"Bye, and thank you again for helping me," the older woman said as she was led away and seated in a special glassed off section for prestige class passengers, right next to the light brown-haired woman who'd left her in the dust.

Mother and daughter? A family resemblance certainly wasn't visible.

Traveling companion or caregiver? Amy didn't think so. The clothes the light brunette wore shouted designer quality.

Amy studied the younger woman. She had Nordic features with high cheeks, wide set eyes, and the long, trim body of a swimmer. Not at all like the older woman.

Amy hated being critical, especially of strangers. She liked to give people the benefit of doubt, but she couldn't help herself and squinted with disapproval.

That second look triggered a memory. Something about the younger woman seemed vaguely familiar, but Amy couldn't place the connection. It would come to her…eventually. She never forgot a face.

****

Gage Townsend witnessed the whole event. What was the matter with his fiancé? The selfishness of her actions surprised him. A shiver of frustration rippled through him. He'd let a lot of little things pass. As the wedding drew closer, Trudy grew more on edge and, he wondered if her fits of temper were a ploy to cancel their engagement.

Why was he engaged to her? Convenience? He didn't think so. They'd practically grown up together with their mothers being best friends.

Oh, he knew. Didn't need a reminder. Their parents wanted to merge the two family businesses—Dream Devices and Cyber Technology—into one gigantic corporation. Their engagement reminded him of an archaic combining of noble houses.

Which it was!

Still, he frowned. He'd trailed his mother and Trudy, only to have another female passenger stand and slip behind them. He slowed his pace, enjoying the sway of her slender body clad in blue jeans and bulky turquoise sweater as she tried to traverse the narrow hall on the moving train without bumping into the walls. Not an easy trick.

When Trudy shot past his mother, he'd started to call her out. Only to clamp his lips tight when the third woman, a total stranger, offered his mother a helping hand.

Reaching the dining car, he spotted Trudy and his mother seated at the far end. The stranger stood waiting for a place to open at one of the tables, which were packed full. It would be a while by his guess.

"Mr. Townsend, how nice to see you. I'll take you to your table. Please follow me," the hostess greeted him.

He snuck a glance at the woman beside him. "This lady is before me."

Sapphire blue eyes with the slightest hue of pink blinked at him. "That's all right. I'm waiting for a seat to open."

Gage didn't waste a breath. "Then eat with us. I owe you for what you did for my mother. It's the least I can do."

She stepped back as though reluctant. "Oh, I couldn't impose."

He cupped her elbow, and was surprised at the heat rushing up his arm from the touch, and how much he enjoyed the sensation. "Nonsense. I insist. I'm Gage Townsend... You are?"

"Amy Phillips."

He didn't see any wedding rings on her left hand. "Well, it's a pleasure to meet you, Miss Philipps, and I'm sure my mother will be delighted to learn the name of her door champion."

A dimpled smile revealed itself. "Well, I am hungry. Thank you. And call me Amy."

"All my pleasure."

At the prestige table, his mother beamed a huge smile of approval. "I should have invited you myself. Glad my son has manners."

Trudy studied his guest with a frown pulling shapely eyebrows together. He tensed, worried she would create a scene about inviting a stranger to join them.

A second of quiet passed. Maybe he misjudged. Tight muscles lessened. "You've already met my mom, Lottie Townsend and this is my fiancé, Trudy Blankenship."

"Do I know you?" Trudy asked.

****

Amy did a double-take. No wonder familiarity had tickled her brain earlier. The grating voice brought back memories she'd filed under 'do not open'. Her college nemesis stared her square in the face.

Princess Trudy.

The old nickname popped into her head without any trouble and Amy gulped.

That settled it. Determination spiked through her. If she experienced doubts about accepting Gage's offer to dinner, she changed her mind on the spot.

Amy claimed the seat next to the window and placed a napkin in her lap. "Trudy Blankenship. I'm crushed. You don't recognize me? We attended Wellesley together. I must admit we haven't seen each other since graduation."

"Amy Phillips," Trudy replied, sipping red wine, green eyes hard. "What are you doing on the train?"

Amy offered her friendliest, most professional realtor smile. It made sense the handsome man would be attached to the ex-beauty queen. What did surprise her was the flash of disappointment that he picked such a conceited example of a human being. "Riding it, like you. I'm on vacation. Going to Banff to take in the winter sights. I've never been there before."

Trudy shrugged as if unimpressed. "I've been coming since I was a child. This is probably my fifteenth or twentieth trip. I've lost count. I used to ski with my parents, but since dad hurt himself, he doesn't ski anymore."

Amy never backed down from a confrontation. She thrived on it. Trudy and she weren't friends in college. Far from it. Though they did share a few classes. Being a scholarship kid and

Trudy rolling in old money didn't make for chummy companions.

"Weren't you the lucky one," she said, instantly wishing she could take back her words. Trudy's silence was worse than any mean come back she could have uttered.

"Do you ski?" Mrs. Townsend asked.

Amy laughed, willing to go along with the distraction. "Used to. Took lessons, bought season lift tickets. The whole shebang. I tried for a couple years, but driving up to Snoqualmie Pass in bad weather with icy and snowy roads gave me a white-knuckle syndrome. I do love snow though."

A waitress handed them menus and asked if they would like a drink.

"A Riesling for me," Gage answered. "What would you care for, Amy?"

"Riesling sounds good. Thank you."

"I like snow too," he added, after ordering a glass for both of them. "It makes everything look so different. Almost magical."

"Like nature's costume party," Amy answered him.

Gage's smile lit up their confined area. "That's it. A perfect description."

Trudy tossed her a smoldering glare. What bothered her? Surely, she wasn't jealous that her fiancé agreed with her about snow. How petty. He was only being nice because she'd aided his mother.

Lottie Townsend smiled. "Where are you staying, Amy?"

"At the Banff Fairmont Springs."

"Us too. I hope you brought your swimsuit. The outdoor hot springs are fabulous. Once, I was there and it began to snow and was so beautiful." Lottie touched her head. "Plus, I wasn't the only one with grey hair. Mine started turning in my late teens, but the freezing temperature turned everyone's white."

Trudy set her wine glass down on the table with a thud. "It's a big hotel. And we'll be busy checking out venues for our wedding. I doubt Amy has interest in that."

Gage hissed and leaned forward ever so slightly. "That's enough, Trudy."

Her green eyes widened in mock innocence. "What? I'm telling the truth. We're going to be extremely busy over the next few days."

The awkward situation needed diffusing. "Awesome," Amy said. "When's the happy event?"

Before anyone could utter an answer, their waitress stopped at the table with their drinks and to take their orders.

After the waitress left, small talk was exchanged. Whenever Trudy spoke, snide comments poured out of her mouth— sleeping conditions on the train were not up to her standards, too many people crowded the dome cars, and the rocking motion drove her nuts. Princess Trudy had turned into a troll.

Thankfully, it didn't take long for their meals to arrive and talk to dwindle. Gage ate fast, as if in a hurry for dinner to end. Amy fidgeted, wanting to ask Trudy why she choose to travel by train if she found it inconvenient, but held her tongue.

Finishing a scoop of orange sherbet for dessert, Amy rose and thanked Gage for allowing her to join them.

Gage stood, and so did his mother. Both smiled. Trudy glared at them, none-too-pleased, but Amy merely shrugged. The tall, green-eyed woman better get used to compromise if she planned on marrying. Instinct told her that Gage Townsend would only tolerate so much guff before he put his foot down and she predicted if Trudy didn't have an attitude adjustment, divorce loomed in her future.

The foursome made their way out of the crowded dinner car. Amy noticed Gage always positioned himself to hold the doors.

At her berth, she ducked out of the aisle. Trudy rushed past without as much as a wave or good-bye.

The snub slid right off her and she volunteered a genuine smile. "Once again, thank you for inviting me to dinner. It was delightful."

Lottie wrapped her in a hug. "It was a sincere pleasure. Please, let's do this again at the Fairmont."

"Mom's right. We need to do this again."

Well over six feet, Gage Townsend towered over her. She'd always been attracted to taller men. His coal-black hair looked like it would never thin, and his eyes were the darkest brown she'd ever seen. His features were sharp, but not pointed. Just enough roundness to soften his face. His weight balanced his height perfectly, and she suspected rock hard muscles lay beneath his clothes.

When he held out his hand to shake hers, her skin burned at his touch. Warm. Hot. Her pulse thrummed with excitement.

What was the matter with her? She was crushing on a man already taken. Hadn't history taught her that wasn't a good idea?

Chapter Two

"Sit back and enjoy the ride," the driver of the lime green and silver bus announced in the parking lot alongside the train station. "You're in for a treat. The drive from Jasper to Banff on the Columbia Icefields Parkway takes a little over three hours. Longer if we stop to let people take photos. It's one of the top scenic trips you'll ever take in your lifetime."

Amy spotted a sleek, black limo with darkly tinted windows accelerate from the parking lot. A little hitch pinched her heart. Probably Gage and his party.

"Isn't this exciting," said the middle-aged woman sitting next to Amy. She was bundled in a fuzzy white hat, a parka that went to her knees and black boots halfway up her legs. "This is my first trip to Banff, but I'm staying a couple days at Lake Louise before I go there."

Amy smiled. "I've heard it's beautiful. This is my first trip, too, but I'm going straight to Banff."

"I can hardly wait. Lake Louise for relaxation. Then Banff. So many things on my to-do list—the gondola ride, seeing the northern lights, sleigh rides, and shopping in town. Have you ever heard of ammonite? It's some kind of opal-like fossil that is found only here. People turn it into beautiful jewelry."

Amy's ears perked up. Though she couldn't afford uber expensive pieces, jewelry was something she had a fondness for. "No, I haven't, but it sounds interesting. I'll look for it. Thanks for the tip."

Her companion grinned. "Hope I can afford a nice piece. The ones with blue or red are considered the best. I've got so many grandkids to bring souvenirs home for. Just little stuff, but it all adds up."

"They're lucky to have you as a grandma."

The bus driver cranked the ignition and the big engine purred. The bus merged with traffic. Snow and ice covered the road. The bus's speed increased. Amy couldn't believe how fast they were traveling. It had to be well over the speed limit. Complaining was out, so she gritted her teeth and held on to the edge of her seat for dear life.

"Take a look on either side of the bus," the driver said over an intercom after a few minutes. "This forest belongs to the world's largest boreal forest. It covers nearly sixty percent of Canada and stretches from Newfoundland and Labrador to the northern Yukon. There are pockets so dense that sunlight can't reach the ground. It makes for an unhealthy forest. You've heard of the pine beetle, haven't you?"

Amy's traveling companion shook her head, her fluffy hat bobbing up and down. Other passengers reacted to the spiel by sharing a questioning look with each other.

The driver went on, "The mountain pine beetle is a species of bark beetle native to our forests. It destroys whole areas of lodge pole pine. We have a current outbreak in our national parks which has caused the destruction of millions of acres. That's good and bad. Bad because it destroys the trees, but good because sometimes the forest needs open space to grow."

Amy wondered if Gage's limo driver delivered the same pitch. Had he visited Banff before? He never said and it made her curious.

The bus driver cleared his throat. "The area between Jasper and Banff is known for thermal activity. The closer we get to Lake Louise and Banff, you'll see frozen rivers with open water. The thermal activity keeps ice from forming, which gives the wildlife a place to find fresh water."

By the murmurs from passengers, they hadn't considered the possibility and approved of the idea that nature took care of its own.

The breadth and beauty of the peaks just got better and better as the bus ate up the miles. It made Amy question the violent turmoil it took to create such a landscape. She looked from left to right so often her neck developed a crick in it. Too much to capture in a single trip. She mentally vowed to return.

The thought elicited a smile. She'd grown used to the bus's speed and let the motion lull her into a relaxed state. Her eyes drifted closed until the driver interrupted again.

"Look to the right, folks. We're passing Glacier Skywalk. It offers walks on a glass platform that extends over a two hundred foot drop. Personally, I don't approve of the monstrosity in the national park, but no one asked me for my opinion."

"Government," someone up front said in a voice loud enough for everyone to hear.

Several laughed.

A little longer into the trip, the driver made another announcement. "We're coming up to the Athabasca Glacier. Normally we would stop, but a heavy snowfall the other day has made stopping treacherous. We might get stuck. Sorry about that."

A black limo sat stationary in the parking lot. The same one Amy saw at the train station? Her heart fluttered. Two people stood at the rim facing the glacier—a woman in a pink outfit that made her look like a frozen popsicle of pink lemonade and a man with broad shoulders in a ski shell pointing to something on the ground.

In seconds the bus sped on. A tiny spike of regret filled Amy. If that had been Gage Townsend, she would have been secretly thrilled to run into him.

Taken, taken, taken.

Amy chanted the mantra to remind herself that he was off-limits.

The driver continued to interrupt with monologues about the area, the welfare of the wild animals, and the national parks. By mid-afternoon they turned onto a road that went up a mountainside. He announced, "Lake Louise coming up."

****

Gage sat in silence for the remainder of the drive to Banff. He couldn't get Amy Phillips out of his mind, which was totally out of character for him. Something about the petite brunette struck a chord deep inside him. He was a good judge of people and her natural spunk shone through loud and clear. Plus, she had to be smart to attend Wellesley.

He glanced at his fiancé. Trudy dozed. They'd stopped at the glacier in hopes of catching sight of big horn sheep. The wind off the dense ice field had chilled him to the bone and invigorated him. Not Trudy. She'd complained about the cold the whole time they'd ventured outside. A winter wedding wasn't her idea and she'd hated losing the argument, but her parents had out-voted her.

His mother laid her hand on his arm. "You okay? You've been awfully quiet."

"Lots on my mind."

"I can imagine. Getting married is a big step, even for you." His mother shifted closer to whisper, "Are you suffering wedding jitters?"

He closed his eyes for a moment and the image of striking blue eyes in a dimpled face popped into his head. The intensity threw him for a loop. Opening his eyes, he studied his mother as he raked his hair off his brow. "You worried about me? That I'll back out?"

"I'm your mother. I will always worry about you. But backing out—heaven's no."

"Good. Glad that's out of the way."

He looked out the window, pretending to admire the scenery. He could fantasize about Amy Phillips all he wanted.

Not that anything would come of it. Pursing her was out of the question. His commitment to Trudy—while not his favorite—came first and he didn't believe in breaking vows. He'd been raised to honor his word.

His mother leaned back into the cushions of the limo. "We haven't really discussed the wedding. Do you have any preconceived ideas about what you want?"

"Not really. I always assumed it and all the frou-frou was for the bride. I know Trudy isn't happy about having the wedding here, but it's important to her parents, so she's going along with their wishes. You can't accuse her of being a selfish daughter."

After a long silence, his mother said, "Her mother and I have been best friends for over thirty years. Helen might have spoiled Trudy, but she did teach her to obey. In the meantime, all I want is for you to be happy."

"I am happy." He squeezed her hand and dropped the subject.

****

Amy stayed on the bus and admired the icicles, some three feet long and as thick as a man's arm, trimming the eves of the Lake Louise hotel while several couples and her companion, disembarked. They gathered their baggage and disappeared into the grand structure.

The iconic hotel was a heritage site. In preparation for her trip, she'd searched the internet and requested pamphlets and literature from every establishment to read about the places, this one included. She was old-fashioned like that.

To think the hotel started as a one-story log cabin in the eighteen hundreds to host visitors from railway stations and day visitors from Banff. Boy, had it changed, morphing into a place accommodating over five hundred guests.

Her only regret was Lake Louise which gave the area its name was blocked by the sprawling hotel.

The driver returned to the bus and restarted the engine. The bus rumbled to life and moved away.

Banff, here, she came.

Amy pulled a fistful of shiny brochures from her tote and began reading them for the umpteenth time as the bus rolled around the circular driveway and headed down the steep road. The gondola ride looked tempting. She'd never ridden in one, and was curious and apprehensive at the same time. A mild phobia of heights was something she was determined to beat. When she'd learned to ski, she'd taken the lift but never the one to the summit. The pamphlet of Banff's gondola showed a much higher ride, elevation 7,486 feet above sea-level.

Pictures of the alpine town showed plenty of stores to keep her occupied with window shopping. Several jewelry stores. Hopefully, one would carry a selection of ammolite. How she'd missed knowing the area was famous for the semi-precious gemstone was beyond her.

She eyed a year-round Christmas store. A two-storied wonder called The Spirit of Christmas. A definite stop on her list. She planned to buy an ornament with the year to add to her collection.

One pamphlet mentioned a distillery that was the only licensed one in the world in a national park. They provided free tours. She wondered if a tasting room existed. That deserved investigating. Not that she was a big drinker.

The Fairmont brochure listed restaurants, shops, and featured several outdoor activities—skiing, canyon walks with frozen waterfalls, and caving—to keep her days full.

Full enough to avoid Gage Townsend.

Chapter Three

Gage spent time emptying his suitcase after arriving at Banff. Because his mother traveled with Trudy and him, they'd reserved three separate suites. Not that his mother was a prude. It just made sense at the time.

Trudy told him she planned to browse the hotel stores after unpacking. He caught the underlying message—she was going shopping—one of her favorite pastimes.

On impulse, he'd told her to put whatever she found in the boutiques on his room tab. A guilty conscience speaking for spending so much time thinking about Amy Phillips?

Possibly.

Shrugging, he tried to dismiss the thought.

His offer had been sincere and generated a big, smacking kiss from his fiancé. Too bad it sparked no response on his end.

His mother went to nap.

He finished unpacking. What now? Hunt for Trudy? Not necessary. All three had agreed to meet for dinner in the Banffshire Club to discuss how to proceed with their plans for the next few days.

Instead, he headed for the Castle Pantry next to registration. A cup of black coffee would perk him up. His one habit—whether good or bad—was coffee. A chemical juggernaut that he loved. Caffeine could be infused directly into his blood stream and he'd be a happy man.

The lobby was decked out for the holidays. Wreaths festooned windows and a twenty-foot evergreen tree stood in a corner and soared to the ceiling. It was covered in red balls with red poinsettias ringing the branches, golden lanterns, and zillions of tiny white lights. The tree was real if the fresh pine scent filling the air was any indication. All the arches in the hotel wore garlands of artificial greenery, lights, and poinsettias.

Gage loved Christmas, the lights, the decorations, the music, and the way people smiled wider. Everyone seemed friendlier at this time of the year. Watching them go about their business always made him smile and he took a seat to sip his coffee while he enjoyed the view.

The pitter-patter of little feet echoed in the lobby. A toddler, maybe two or three, ran across the lustrous sheen of marble, chubby fingers stretching upward to a model of the hotel when a woman's voice hollered not to touch. His gaze stayed on the child. Her arm dropped but the glow on the cherub-like face said it all.

She stared at the replica on a table by the double doors. Tiny plastic windows aglow from within and Christmas trees sat on each corner of the structure. An over-sized snowman, not to scale, rested on the roof of the first floor.

A woman stopped beside the child.

The toddler pointed. "Tanta's house, Mama."

"Yes, Sweetie. We'll look closer later. First, we need to find our room."

The reunion pinched Gage's heart. He and Trudy hadn't discussed kids yet. He wondered what her take on them was. A number of topics needed to be to aired before the actual wedding.

Shaking himself out of the melancholy mood, he glanced out-of-doors. Snow fluttered in the air. Nature was decorating the terrain with a fresh coating.

An elderly bell-hop approached. His white hair stuck out from his cap in all different directions as though he forgot to comb it that morning. "Can I refresh your cup, sir?"

"I'm good for now. Thanks."

"As you wish, sir. Ole Sam will fix you right up with whatever you need. Everyone at the Fairmont wants your stay to be the best experience."

With a courteous smile, the bell-hop bobbed his head and proceeded toward the archway leading to the row of shops. Gage swore the man whistled.

A lime green and silver tour bus rolled to a stop at the front. People started disembarking and his heartrate increased. Maybe this was the bus that Amy Phillips had taken. He'd seen an identical one parked in the lot at the train station. Standing, feeling a flutter of excitement, he walked to the front doors in hopes it was hers.

****

Arriving at her destination, Amy gawked out the bus window. She stuffed the brochures back in her tote. She'd learned so much about the hotel and area, she could barely contain her excitement to start her long, over-due vacation.

The Fairmont Banff surpassed all expectations. Another hotel built to increase tourism of the Canadian west and traffic on the railways. Like at Lake Louise, several fires destroyed the original hotel. Each time it had been rebuilt, bigger and better, culminating with the current façade.

It even stayed open during the Great Depression. People had wanted to live life to the fullest and the hotel provided just such a destination. Only during World War II had it closed for three years.

She waited her turn to retrieve her suitcase from the luggage compartment and walked through the double doors.

"Amy! Amy!"

Inside the spacious lobby, someone called her name. She spotted Gage Townsend's huge strides gobbling the distance between them. He stopped before her and eased her stroller suitcase from her grip. Just seeing him gave her a thrill.

Why were the good ones always taken?

One affair was enough to last her a lifetime. In self-defense, she hadn't known the man was married until after she'd fallen head-over-heels in love. It broke her heart to end the relationship, but her life had no room for cheaters.

Dark brown eyes beamed down at her. "Welcome to the Castle in the Rockies."

"What are you doing here? I—I mean...in the lobby. I know you're staying at the hotel." Embarrassment ripped through her in a hot wave. She was a realtor, for heaven's sake. She was supposed to be quick on her feet. Intelligent responses always tripped from her mouth.

Gage grinned at her. "I was just sitting in the lobby enjoying a cup of coffee when I spotted the bus. Thought I recognized it from the train station. Decided to wait and see if you were on it." His smile widened. "And you were. My lucky day."

A buzzing grew louder as people stopped to admire the interior or streamed on either side of them, rushing to the registration desk to check in.

Amy wasn't sure what to make of Gage's greeting. The man was engaged, spoken-for, off-limits, in her mind. "Appreciate the welcome. Where's Trudy and your mom?"

"Mother is resting. While she'll never admit it, traveling by train was hard on her. She needs a hip replacement, but refuses to slow down. Plus, it was her idea and I couldn't refuse her. This is her second visit to Banff and she always dreamed of returning. Plus, she wanted to be involved with the wedding plans. Trudy is shopping. It keeps her happy and the hotel has over a dozen shops."

His words contained an undercurrent Amy couldn't quite put her finger. "I imagine Trudy has a lot of practice shopping. In college she always wore the best outfits, setting fashion trends everyone envied."

"I didn't peg you for the envious type."

"In all honesty, I admired her outfits, but had the good sense not to emulate her. My budget couldn't afford the hit." Amy stared at Gage. "I did beat her in debate. I confess, that was fun. But I'll deny saying that if you tell her."

Her comment drew a huge smile from the tall man. "It'll be our secret. Knowing Trudy, I bet she wasn't happy. She's very competitive and likes winning too much."

An uneasy quiver rippled through her body as she stood in the lobby disparaging Trudy and she felt obligated to speak up. "Oh, she handled it fairly well. I mean, she didn't throw anything at me." Then she remembered her jalopy of a car had been keyed in the parking lot a few days later. Even after all this time, she wondered if Trudy had been the culprit.

She glanced at the reception area. The check-in line shrank fast. "It was nice talking to you, but I need to register, Gage. I plan to check out Banff before it gets too dark. I've got a couple hours before the stores close."

He backed away, as if embarrassed. "Sure. Sure. I didn't mean to disturb you." He wheeled her suitcase to the front desk. "We'll see you around, I'm sure. My mother really enjoyed your company on the train."

Warmth spiraled from Amy's toes to the tips of her ears. "You thank her for me. Bye," she said, turning to the clerk behind a slab of marble countertop.

The dark-haired woman smiled. "Welcome to the Fairmont Banff."

"Thank you. I'm looking forward to my stay here."

"Just watch out for the ghosts." The clerk winked. "We have several famous ones on the premise. A missing room where a whole family—father, mother, and their two children—were murdered. To this day, guests hear screams echo in hallways and bloody handprints appear on mirrors."

Amy shuddered. "Spooky."

"It's not as bad as it sounds. We have friendly ghosts, too. Keep an eye out for Samuel McCauley. He was a Scotsman employed his whole life at the Fairmont. Rumor has it when he sickened, he refused to quit and showed up every day with a smile, ready for duty. Never late. Never missed a day. Management, feeling obligated for his years of service, allowed him to continue. He died in his bed on the staff level. Every so often, people swear he greets them in the lobby, takes their luggage, and escorts them to their room."

Amy had a hard time swallowing the far-fetched tale. "Is that where Casper, the friendly ghost came from?"

"Oh, no. Casper was created in the late 1930s. This happened in 1975."

****

Gage left the lobby. He had never stood in a hotel, much less anywhere, to waylay an attractive woman, and dump about Trudy. That wasn't his style or who he was. It bothered him that he couldn't stop feeling critical of his fiancé. He could only imagine how small he appeared in Amy's blue eyes.

He hurried under the arch leading to the popular shops, then skidded to an abrupt stop. What the hell was the matter with him?

"Anything wrong, sir," the bell-hop Sam interrupted his inner soliloquy. "You look upset. Is there anything I can assist you with?"

Gage almost requested a stiff drink. "No, Sam, but thanks for the offer. Maybe another time."

The elderly man bowed his head. "Just think of me and I'll appear."

"Sounds good." With a nod Gage turned away, mildly puzzled by the odd answer. He took a couple steps, then turned to where he'd left Sam. The man was gone.

What was going on?

Scratching his head, Gage frowned. A sexy stranger. Disappearing bell-hops. This trip was turning into a number of firsts.

Rather than search for Trudy, he sought his mother. He suspected she'd appreciate being informed of Amy's arrival and headed for the elevators.

On their floor, he rapped on the door to her suite.

"Coming," came a sleepy voice.

The door opened. "Mom, I didn't mean to wake you."

She scrubbed her face. "It was time. I wouldn't be able to sleep tonight if I rested much longer. What's up?"

"Nothing. Thought I'd check on you." He entered and sat in one of the stuffed, padded chairs next to the window. The scene through the glass panes appeared almost dream-like. A blanket of white turned the land into a winter wonderland. In the distance, as dusk fell, Banff began to sparkle with the glow of Christmas and night-time lights.

She snorted. "Since when do I need checking on? Something on your mind."

"Guess I was lonely. Trudy's off shopping and that's not my favorite appropriation of time."

"You promised to take me to the Christmas store."

"I make exceptions for Christmas." He grinned wide. "I went for a cup of coffee and ran into Amy Phillips checking into the hotel."

"You just happened to be in the lobby? Convenient."

"Mom, I don't need your sarcasm right now. There's a lot to process."

"Sorry. I know it's not business you're processing. Cyber Tech is doing great. Must be the wedding. Marriage is a lifetime commitment. Having second thoughts? It happens to the best of men."

He raised his brows. "Thanks for the reminder. That's the second time you mentioned me having doubts. What's up?"

A twinkle lit his mother's eyes as she shook off the vestiges of her nap. "It's not like you to doubt yourself. Do you want to talk about it?"

"We are talking."

"In circles…"

Talking with his mother—frustration surfaced again. He suffered a twinge of guilt at questioning himself. Did he even know what he wanted? "Let it go, Mom." He looked away to gather his thoughts. Darkness fell fast in the northern latitude during winter time. City lights glowed in all their glory. The scene of snow, lights, and stars seemed magical. "Disappointed?"

His mother chuckled. "With you? Never. If it's the wedding. Need I remind you that Trudy's a good woman. Spoiled, but I blame Helen for that. Give Trudy time, she'll settle down."

Pressure weighed on him. He let his voice soften. "I know."

She finger-combed her short white hair. A weary resolve settled on her face. "You're not getting ideas about anyone else, are you? Say Amy Phillips? That might be a bad idea."

Gage laughed. "You know me better than that. I would never do anything to hurt Trudy's feelings."

****

Amy rode the Blue Line bus from downtown Banff to the Fairmont. As she stared out the window into the darkness that fell in the last two hours, the image of Gage Townsend appeared in the reflection of the glass. She didn't want to think about him, but couldn't seem to stop herself. He seemed so nice, and he was definitely handsome. It wasn't fair the good ones were always taken.

When she exited the bus, the temperature had dropped to well below freezing. Every breath drew in icy daggers as she hurried from the bus stop into the warmth of the hotel. Her foray into town had been worth the trip. She'd found the perfect ammolite necklace—an oval pendant with hints of blue and red about an inch wide on a silver chain, and the price fit her budget, which she appreciated.

She rushed to the elevator, determined to enjoy a dip in the hot springs before eating a late dinner or maybe treating herself to room service. Thank heaven she'd thrown a swimsuit into her suitcase. In her room, she changed clothes, tossed on a hotel robe, and used the provided slippers to make her way to the pool area.

When she reached the pool, humid air smacked her face. After the wintery blast in town it came as a surprise. Stripping her robe, she folded and set it on one of the chaise lounges circling an Olympic-size indoor pool. The hot springs were outside. Plastic strips kept the worst of the chilly air from invading the room. She ducked between the strips and gasped.

Several young men—college students on Christmas break—stood in the pool near the entrance and chuckled at her reaction. One had an armful of tattoos. She remembered her father telling her brother when he joined the Navy, not to come home if he got a tattoo. He didn't.

Did Gage? She shook her head. She had to stop thinking about him.

"I wasn't expecting the temperature extremes," she replied in way of explanation to the young men.

Steam billowed from the water like flimsy streamers as the college students' shifted positions in the pool. The squeals of two adolescent girls, children really, filled the star-studded night. They floated and splashed on foam noodles. A man and woman clung to the side, engrossed with each other. Three men with their backs to the entrance were in an animated discussion at a far corner.

Amy laughed and slipped into the water. "I didn't expect the air to be so cold."

The closest college student nodded. "The pool heats you real fast."

He wasn't kidding. Almost instantly, steamy water chased away the night's freezing temperature. She floated toward the deep end, letting the hot springs relax muscles. When she reached her destination, a young girl clung to the side as if afraid to move.

"Where's your parents?" Amy hoped the child wasn't left alone with a group of strangers. That would be bad parenting in her book.

The girl nodded toward the three men. "Daddy's over there."

As if his name had been uttered, a man with a dad-belly turned, parent radar on alert hearing his daughter speak with a stranger.

Relief bloomed in Amy. She turned her attention back to the girl. "Can you swim?"

"I haven't passed my swimming test yet."

She nodded. "I'm not a very good swimmer myself. I don't like putting my face in the water, so I learned to swim like a frog."

"What's that?"

"It's a form of swimming called the breaststroke. You swim on your chest and most of the time your head is out of the water. Your arms pulls you through the water and your legs perform a frog kick. Want me to show you?" At the girl's nod, Amy kicked off from the wall.

She stopped swimming next to the man and woman, found the bottom, and turned around to face the little girl. "Your turn. Be a frog."

"No, no. I can't."

"Sure you can. Just pretend you're a frog."

The man muttered under his breath. While Amy didn't catch his exact words, she was positive he cussed in a foreign language. Obscenities never needed translation. Something upset him. Glaring at her, after a moment, the couple sloshed out of the pool.

Frowning at their behavior, Amy shrugged and turned her attention back to the girl. "Come on, sweetie. You can do it. Swim like a frog."

All it took was encouragement. The young girl inhaled a deep breath and pushed off the wall. She thrashed her arms, holding her head out of the water, and kicked with all her might. When she came abreast of Amy, a huge grin lit her face. "I did it. I'm a frog, too. Daddy…daddy, did you see? I can swim."

Dad-belly waved. "You're doing great, Kandi."

Amy smiled, glad to have made the girl happy. "Now, let's see if we can find you a swim noodle."

"Take mine," said one of the college students who first spoke to her. "I'm done."

One of the teenage girls swam up to them, pushing a noddle. "We're leaving, too. You can have mine."

"You sure? Thanks."

Abandoned swimming noodles bobbed in the pool.

Amy and Kandi floated in the warm water. With each kick, steam rose into the night air. Amy remembered Lottie Townsend saying everyone's hair turned white and she was right. There wasn't a single person in the pool with normal-colored hair.

"You know you insulted that couple," said a familiar voice that sent ripples down Amy's spine.

She sputtered, thrashing in the water to find her footing. "What? What do you mean?"

Dad-belly accompanied Gage Townsend. "Afraid he's correct, Miss. That couple who left in a huff were French Canadian. The reason they stomped out was because they didn't appreciate being called frogs. It's a holdout from the past. There are three popular theories that I know of. The first one is because they enjoy *cuisses de grenouilles*—frog legs. That came from long ago when British soldiers poked fun at them and called them frog-eaters, which was shortened to frogs.

"The second one comes from World War II when French soldiers were so adept at camouflage that they were difficult to find when under cover. That's a compliment, but they didn't like the reference to frogs." The man shifted in the pool, freeing steam into the air. "The last theory came from Clovis I, the first king of the Franks. His banner had three toads on it, but they replaced with the *Fleur-de-lis*."

"Oh, I feel awful."

"You don't have to worry about it. I'm a minister and Canadian, too. My countrymen on the east coast are overly sensitive. Besides, I thought it was hilarious, and God has already forgiven you."

Amy listened to the condescending explanation. He probably came from British stock, like most Canadians. Still, embarrassment scorched her cheeks. "Nonetheless, I might have hurt their feelings. That wasn't my intent."

Chapter Four

Gage approved of the sight of Amy standing in the hotel hot springs in her plain, one-piece navy-blue bathing suit. It fit slender curves to perfection. He'd seen her enter the pool, but decided not to intrude. Probably because he knew if he wasn't in a relationship, he would seriously consider asking her for a date.

Whoa! Down boy.

Gage swallowed an unsteady breath, then tottered backward as if distance would rid his head of her bewitching appeal. Why was he so attracted to a woman he'd met less than twenty-four hours ago? Spent, at the most, two hours with.

"Have you eaten dinner yet, Amy?" He faced her. "I was just getting ready to leave. Mom, Trudy, and I have reservations at 7:30 p.m. We'd be thrilled to have you join us."

"That's thoughtful, Gage. But I haven't even unpacked. I raced off to Banff first thing. Maybe another night?"

What the heck was the matter with him? He had no business pursuing the woman. He was engaged. "Sure. Whenever it's convenient?"

The minister and his daughter climbed out of the pool.

Gage should do the same himself, but leaving wasn't what his heart wanted. Instead, he stood like a fool gawking at Amy.

She stared up at him, dimples showing. "You should see yourself. Your hair is white, but it looks good on you."

He patted his head, felt the stiffness. "Thanks. It's crunchy. You, too. Someday, you'll make a beautiful grandmother."

"Your mom was right. Tell her I said so."

Her deflection impressed him. He was even more impressed with the woman herself. She'd been kind to spend time with the young girl. Something he seriously doubted Trudy would have done.

Amy had turned down his dinner invitation. Disappointed, he still considered it a smart move on her part. Now all he had to do was hope his feelings of attraction would pass. They had to…

****

Amy clung to the pool noodle with clenched fingers turning into prunes. She wanted to die. Not that it mattered.

Humiliation scorched her for insulting a person in their own country in front of Gage, even if unintentional.

No legitimate reason existed for refusing Gage's dinner invitation, except embarrassment. The man was being polite.

Common sense shouted at her to refuse, and thank heaven she listened.

One affair was all she could handle in a lifetime.

Casting a sidelong glance at his tall muscular frame, she watched him collect loose noodles that people had abandoned. Wow! She never expected to see him do that. A man in his position didn't have to clean up after others. Maybe that was his secret for success. He made sure jobs got done.

She mentally put on her business hat. Dinner wouldn't have been a bad idea. In fact, interacting with Gage Townsend might prove a financial windfall. If she remembered correctly, Cyber Technology's headquarters were located in Seattle, but she'd heard rumors they were considering expanding to others cities in the area. Maybe their meeting could lead to a beneficial business trade. He could send contacts her way. In turn, she could offer his company real estate advice. At least that's what she tried to convince herself.

Or was she jumping the gun, making assumptions?

She'd already passed the broker's test. All she had to do was activate her license and open her own realty office.

Either way, she convinced herself juggling this crazy attraction and a business agreement without becoming romantically involved with the handsome man would be a breeze. Well, maybe a stiff breeze. Certainly not a gale force wind.

Gage's arms overflowed with pool noodles. Before she got ahead of herself, she might as well appreciate the sight of wet trunks clinging to his cute derriere and long muscular legs as he set them on the ground to climb out of the pool. When he bent over to pick up the flotation toys, she sighed, unable to tear her gaze away.

Just one man remained in the pool. After spotting Gage depart, she nodded farewell and headed indoors with her pool noodle.

She grabbed her bathrobe and shuffled in her slippers to a barrel to stuff her noodle inside. She'd unpack, relax, and order room service for her first night in Banff. Staying in her room would eliminate bumping into Gage again.

Doing that made sense.

Not that she was justifying avoiding the handsome businessman.

****

"I ran into Amy Phillips in the outdoor pool," Gage informed Trudy and his mother as he sat in the crowded hotel restaurant later that evening, "She was teaching a little girl how to swim."

"How nice of her," his mother replied.

Trudy's professionally shaped brows arched dramatically. "Isn't that what a parent is supposed to do? Or, at least, pay for swimming lessons."

The response rubbed him wrong. He narrowed his gaze to glower at his fiancé. "What's the matter with you? She was helping a child, being friendly."

"Now, Trudy, don't be judgmental," his mother answered before he blew a cork. "She doesn't know a soul here. She's probably lonely."

Trudy set her fork down, took a split second to straighten the implement on the table cloth before picking up her wine glass. "I hate to disagree with you, Mrs. T, but you didn't know her in college. We shouldn't waste our time associating with her."

"Trudy," Gage uttered her name, swallowing a curse and tightening a grip on his fork.

Trudy's knuckles whitened on the stem of her wine glass. "What? I'm being honest. I thought you liked that about me."

"I do, but sometimes you're not very kind-hearted to someone traveling all alone."

She shot a glance at his mother before staring him down. "I'm not playing tourist guide for her, if that's what you're hinting at. We aren't friends and my opinion hasn't changed. Besides, I've lined up several florist appointments tomorrow that I thought the *three* of us could check out and then eat dinner in town."

He didn't want to make a big deal out of Trudy being nice to Amy. He dropped the subject. "You don't need me to pick out flowers."

"But—but… What will you do?"

"Take Mom to Banff. I promised to accompany her to the Christmas store."

Trudy leaned forward and laid her hand atop his. "I'm sorry I've been such a bear lately. Wedding jitters are making me grumpy. There are dozens of decisions to make and I've never done it before. It's all new to me."

Gage didn't fall for the pity act. Trudy was an expert at it. She'd even played that game at her father's firm when he'd sat in on meetings. His annoyance rose. Did she think to fool him? He reminded himself he was marrying her because their parents wanted to merge their two companies. "It's my first marriage, too. Maybe we're both on edge."

Perhaps sensing his growing irritation, Trudy sighed. "All right. If it'll make you happy, I'll shuffle some appointments around. We can take our gondola ride later in the week. If I do that… I could invite Amy to a spa treatment. We wouldn't have to do a lot of chit-chat. I could tell her I need to relax with someone my own age." She twisted in her chair, covering her mouth as if embarrassed. "Oops, that came out wrong. Of course, Mrs. T, you're more than welcome to join us, if Amy accepts."

"No thanks, Trudy. I don't particularly care for massages. I was never comfortable with a stranger rubbing on me," his mother answered.

"Oh, Mrs. T, don't be silly." Trudy's voice took on an almost baby-like sound. "You might like it."

His mother narrowed her gaze. "Trust me. I won't."

His mother drew a line in the sand and Gage hoped Trudy wouldn't step over it. "Then it's settled. Trudy, you call Amy and set up your spa treatment. Mom, you and I can go into Banff. I know you can spend all day in a Christmas shop and I want to visit the distillery. They've got a restaurant on the premise. We can eat there."

Waiting for the two women to concur with his plan, he decided he could use a stiff drink after dealing with Trudy.

Relief flooded him when she nodded. At least a nuclear bomb hadn't gone off.

****

The next morning Amy grabbed a tray to slowly contemplate bins of bacon, sausage, scrambled eggs, and hashbrowns at the Castle Pantry, a small cafeteria style restaurant off the hotel lobby. Everything smelled greasy. Her stomach rolled.

She finally chose a carton of orange juice, a bowl of oatmeal, and an English muffin. Paying for her meal, she carried her tray and rounded the corner into a room consisting of a dozen tables with chairs. She picked one of the bar height tables and hefted herself onto a stool. A score of other guests were scattered about, eating and talking. She wasn't the only person starting her day off with a quick meal.

She spread out brochures on the tabletop, trying to figure which of her sight-seeing adventures to take first. She hadn't thoroughly investigated Banff in her quick trip yesterday. Focused on jewelry stores for her ammolite souvenir, she missed The Spirit of Christmas store and the Park Distillery, two places she vowed to visit.

"Looks like you have a full day ahead of you, Miss."

Mildly startled, Amy glanced at an elderly bell-hop standing beside her. She hadn't heard him approach. "That's my plan. I went to town last night for a bit, but didn't give it a thorough examination. Can I ask you a favor?" At his nod, she continued, "Since you live here, do you have any recommendations where to start first?"

The man scratched his white hair. "Town is a fine place to start. I'm a window shopper myself. I used to like strolling down the streets and admiring all the holiday decorations. Pop in here and there to warm up if I got too cold. Although I doubt you can go wrong with whatever you decide."

She glanced at the thin brass name tag on his red jacket. Out of the corner of her eye, she noticed a table of four patrons stare at the man. "Thank you, Samuel. My name is Amy. I suppose you're right. Might as well finish what I started and check it off my list."

"A fine idea, Miss." His rheumy gaze widened when she introduced herself. "Amy, you say. Could you be Amy Phillips by any chance?"

"Yes, I am. Why do you ask?"

He beamed and dug into a front pocket. "I have a message for you." He handed her a sealed envelope with an embossed image of the hotel.

Amy accepted the envelope and tipped him a toonie. "Thank you."

Her name was scrawled across the linen paper in big and bold block letters.

A middle-aged couple at the table next to hers stood and carried their tray of dirty plates to a station for retrieval by the wait staff.

When she glanced up to ask Samuel who gave it to him, he had disappeared as suddenly as he had appeared.

Odd. She never heard him approach or leave and her realtor radar was usually pretty sharp when it came to knowing where people stood in a room. She decided it must be because of all the activity in the restaurant.

Breaking the seal, she scanned the contents. Thank heaven she was sitting down, otherwise she might have collapsed. She held an invitation from Trudy Blankenship to meet her tomorrow at the spa for a girl's day. Reservations for a facial, deep tissue massage, and lunch were set to start at 11:00 a.m. and they were her treat.

Suspicion reared its ugly head. Amy narrowed her eyes to study the paper in case something was hidden between the lines. Maybe the paper was laced with poison and she'd die after touching it.

Why was Princess Trudy being nice to her? Extending a peace offering. It didn't make any sense. Had Gage asked Trudy to make the offer? Had his mother?

What the heck was going on?

Amy stared at the invitation. This would take some hard thinking. The princess and she had nothing in common. She tucked the envelope into her purse. Were her flights of fancy about Gage giving her a guilty conscience and making her paranoid?

Chapter Five

The hotel restaurant on the second floor was packed to capacity with hungry patrons and a queue formed beyond the entrance. A constant buzz, clink of utensils, and shuffling of people coming and going filled the room.

"Let's walk to town," Gage suggested, placing his napkin on his plate. He'd eaten a hearty meal of bacon and eggs. Trudy and his mother had chosen lighter fare.

Trudy made a face, but since she wasn't joining him, he dismissed her censure.

His mother's gaze snapped to him, her eyes wide with curiosity. "Why?"

"Fresh air is good for you. Besides, it's downhill the whole way. I won't make you walk back, if you're worried. Because of your dotage, we'll take a cab or Uber back to the hotel."

She smacked him on the arm. "You forget I'm the shopper in this family. We'll see who has the stamina to outlast who."

He liked teasing his mother and grinned as they stood in unison. "I knew you would be up to the challenge."

Trudy rose on tip-toes to kiss him on the cheek. He acknowledged the gesture with a smile. "I really don't know how long we'll be gone. Let's just agree to meet at 6:30 p.m. at the Italian restaurant."

His mother faced Trudy. "You'll have my full attention for the wedding as soon as I've done a bit of shopping."

"No problem, Mrs. T. I'll figure it out. I've arranged transportation through the hotel to drive me to the different florist shops."

With a nod, Gage took his mother's elbow and lead her downstairs to the hotel's double doors. Outside they bundled up with hats and gloves. Crisp mountain air filled his lungs. He breathed in the coldness and savored the icy burn in his lungs.

Cars, vans, and SUVs sped past them.

His mother set a quick pace. She was trying to prove a point, which made him suspect he'd miscalculated issuing the challenge. Too late, he recalled his dad mentioning his mother could marathon shop without stopping, and groaned.

They made good time and within five minutes crossed the bridge to town. Water trickled beneath at a steady pace. They stopped to admire the sight and his mind wondered what plans Amy had for the day. He imagined her participating in one of the several events the hotel offered its guests—cross-country snowshoeing, sleigh rides, skiing, and of all things—caving. Nearly any and everything to keep their guests happy.

On the move again, the closer they drew to town, the more people he spotted out and about. They dressed like them in heavy coats, hats, and gloves. A coffee shop on the corner with holiday decals stenciled on the windows called to him.

"I could use another cup of coffee before we begin your shopping in earnest," he suggested.

His mother smiled. "Hot chocolate for me."

"Whatever your heart desires."

The warmth inside the shop illustrated a vast temperature swing between outside and inside. No one else patronized the shop. He walked to the counter. "One coffee, black, and one hot chocolate."

"Would you like whip cream on the chocolate?" the barista responded in an accent he didn't quite recognize.

He turned to his mother.

She flashed a crooked grin. "The works."

"You heard the lady." He ran his credit card in the reader. "Where are you from?"

The young man gave him a giant grin. "Australia. Me and my mates come every year to ski. You'll run into quite a few of us in town. We all stay at the Sheep Run Hotel."

"Hope you enjoy Canada. It's a beautiful country."

"It certainly is," the fellow said, then added, "It'll be just a moment. Take a seat and I'll bring your drinks when they're ready."

They sat on a leather sofa facing a gas fireplace with flickering flames. Gage recalled childhood days of sitting in their huge kitchen and waiting for his mother to fix him a drink on cold, winter-like days.

The clanks coming from behind the counter where the young man opened a refrigerator, splashed milk into a cup, and flicked a switch were the same sounds as Gage remembered. Hissing came from a stainless steel stem as the barista swirled the cup around. The process was nearly reversed—a switch flicked, the refrigerator door popped as the vacuum broke, something clanked against its side, a shaking, then the swish of whipping cream being added to the top of the cup.

Gage tried to dismiss the sounds as he looked at his mother. Rosy apples glowed on her round face from their brisk walk. "You doing okay?"

"I'm fine. Why do you ask?"

"Just making conversation."

"Here you go," said the barista, bringing their drinks.

"Thank you," he and his mother said at the same time.

Gage held his cup, inhaling a lightly caramelized, almost nutty aroma as he brought the cup to his lips for that first taste. Simply delicious. He sighed and let the addictive brew percolate through his blood stream. Nothing beat a good cup of coffee. Especially in the morning.

"How's your chocolate?" he asked, seeing his mother sip her drink.

"Perfect. Almost as good as my mother used to make."

"Do you want to drink it here or take it with us?"

"Here. I need both hands while I shop. I like to touch the merchandize."

"Guess that means my hands should be empty to carry all your bags."

"I raised you right."

They sat in silence to finish their drinks. Gage closed his eyes and let his mind wander. For the umpteenth time he wondered what Amy was doing on this bright, crisp morning.

A tiny voice whispered, *bad idea.*

****

Amy enjoyed the bus ride to town. She disembarked at the corner near The Spirit of Christmas store. Through large plate-glass windows decorated with Christmas scenes she saw customers milling inside. Considering the early hour, the retailer was definitely a popular stop.

A bell chimed upon her entrance. Trying to decide what to do—browse the store or just select items as she went—the perfect ornament hanging on a tree branch caught her eye. Immediately she wondered why were all the trees in The Spirit of Christmas so tall?

Gritting her teeth, she stretched on tip-toes, fingertips skimming the bottom of a snowflake. So close, so far. But she had to have it. The deep blue background of snow-covered mountains was an exact match to the color in her living room and made for a brilliantly simple keepsake.

Teetering and stretching to her fullest, she wobbled. She leaned toward the tree. Just a bit more and she'd have it.

Then disaster struck. She lost her balance and a squeak escaped. The tree raced to plant itself in her face. She stuck her arm out to break her fall.

Seconds from catastrophe, strong arms wrapped around her waist and pulled her to safety.

"Thank yo—" She turned to issue a heart-felt thanks and a breath trapped in her throat. Gage Townsend's sexy brown eyes stared down at her. Heat rushed from her toes to her cheeks. "I—I mean, thank you. Much appreciate the save."

"All my pleasure."

His deep voice made matters worse. It curled through her veins like a narcotic smoke. She wanted to inhale it into her body.

Lottie Townsend rounded the far side of the tree. "Hello, Amy. Nice to run into you. Isn't this store fantastic? I couldn't wait to visit Banff after seeing the view from the top floor. The lights at night are wonderful."

Whoever said *three was a crowd* had it all wrong. Amy couldn't have been happier to see Mrs. Townsend. "Yes, it is. Christmas is my favorite holiday. The decorations, the music, and the way people just seem nicer during the holidays."

"I absolutely agree with you," the older woman said.

****

Gage hated releasing Amy. Her petite frame fit into his arms perfectly. Soft curves in all the right places and the faint aroma of spring flowers from shampoo came from her hair. God, he ached to dip his head and kiss her.

"I thought you had wedding plans," she said, looking around the store. "Where's Trudy?"

The enticing spell broke with her words. Gage emerged from his haze. "Checking out the florists in the area. Mom wanted to visit town and I was drafted to play porter and carry her packages."

Amy looked at his hands. "I don't see any."

His mother saved him by stepping forward. "This is our first stop. What about you?"

"I was in Banff yesterday for a quick visit. I wanted to look around some more and cross it off my to-do list."

"Join us," his mother said.

Amy shifted back. "I don't want to intrude."

Gage understood her hesitation. The push-pull of attraction he felt whenever they were together was driving him nuts. Maybe she felt the same enticing feeling. Damn. He shouldn't have those kinds of thoughts. The outcome could only lead to disaster.

"You're not. Gage doesn't give good advice. Typical male. He always tells me, 'buy whatever you want,' just like his father. I want an honest opinion."

"Believe me, you would be saving me from putting my foot in my mouth," Gage said, guessing at her worry and crossing his fingers she accepted the offer.

She pursed her lips, glancing from his mother to him. "I can't seem to say no to you."

His heart triple-timed. "If only that were true. I'm always being rebuffed."

A hearty laugh burst from Amy. "You don't fool me, Gage Townsend. I doubt few people say no to you."

His mother crooked her arm with Amy's. "I think we're going to become friends. Now, what were you trying to reach at the top of the tree?"

"Oh!" Amy's eyes widened. "I nearly forgot. That snowflake at the top with the picture of mountains."

Reaching for the ornament gave Gage something to do, rather than standing around like an extra in a movie. "This one. Pretty."

"I collect them for the year. My parents started collecting them when I was born. I've got twenty-nine."

"Does that mean you're twenty-nine?" he asked.

His mother slapped his arm. "For heaven's sake. Don't you know better than ask a woman her age?"

"It's all right, Mrs. Townsend. I don't mind."

"He was raised better than that."

A tiny grin lifted the corners of Amy's mouth as she accepted the ornament. Her fingers brushed his palm and lightning struck. He swore he heard bells ring. His breath caught as Amy took the snowflake to the counter.

His mother continued shopping. She handed him a snow-globe, her favorite collectable, before heading to a table with Christmas themed serving utensils. She picked up a half-dozen peppermint striped spoons.

He followed his mother while sneaking peeks at Amy, a distraction that appealed to him. After concluding her purchase, she surfed a table set with ceramic trees designed by Thomas Kincaid. One ten-inch tree with color changing lights and a moving train seemed to hold her interest longer than the others. She gingerly picked it up and looked underneath as if checking the price. The light in her blue eyes faded as she set the decoration down.

Ten minutes later, while his mother paid for her items, he covertly stole a glance at the bottom of the tree. Sticker price under two hundred dollars. Reasonable.

He held the door until the two women passed through. "I'll be right back. Go ahead without me," he said, lifting the bag with the snow-globe. "I need to get this double bagged."

He returned inside, conducted his business, and issued instructions, then trailed his mother and Amy to a hat store two buildings down the street.

Entering, Jingle Bells played over the intercom. Laughing like giddy teenagers, they were trying on silly hats. His mother settled on a fluffy Cossack creation, paid for it, and handed him the bag.

Outside again, they checked a window with children's clothes.

"Look at that little girl's dress," Amy said. "It's darling."

Her voice contained a note of longing. After witnessing her interplay with the girl in the pool, he didn't need to ask whether or not she wanted kids. When the right man came along, she would carry his children with a mother's unrelenting love.

Gage stumbled on the sidewalk. A twinge of jealously sparked inside him… Because it wouldn't be with him. Cold sweat raced down his spine.

What was the matter with him?

Before an answer could form his mother pointed. "Have you noticed the snowmen in front of the stores are made of real snow?"

"I have. The town goes all out with their holiday decorations."

It took all morning to peruse the stores on one side of the street. Amy willingly followed his mother into every jewelry, clothing, and nick-knack store she insisted upon investigating. True to her word, his mother could shop. She found a pair of snow boots for herself, a baseball cap with Banff embroidered on it for his father, and a AAA necklace of rainbow ammolite set in gold that put a dent on her credit card. Amy showed them her new pendant and searched for a matching pair of earrings, but didn't have any luck.

Somewhere along the way his mother's pace slowed. Maybe to stretch out the day. Maybe because she was thorough in her shopping. He didn't care. Every extra minute with Army was worth it in his book.

At the corner, they waited for the light to turn green. Traffic whizzed by on the street. He glanced at his watch. Nearly noon.

"Almost time for lunch, ladies," he announced. "The Park Distillery is just up the block. I suggest we stop there for a bite to eat."

His mother beamed. "An excellent idea. I'm starved."

"I read up on the place." Amy's dimples flashed when she grinned. "They're the only licensed distillery in the world in a national park. They make small batches of handmade vodka and whiskey. It's on my 'to see' list."

"I'm here to serve and please."

His mother cast a swift glance at him when the light changed and they crossed the street. He recognized that look and expected a grilling from her later on.

A whiff of alcohol floated down the street as they approached. He opened the door to the distillery and a small retail shop greeted them, not the sour nuances of fermenting grain he had expected. Either restaurant odors camouflaged the normal compounds released in the still as it heated up or they conducted the distillation off premises.

"Let's eat first, then come back," his mother suggested.

The clerk smiled. "That's a good idea. Bring your receipt and receive a ten percent discount."

All three smiled and waited for a table in the crowded restaurant which took a couple minutes.

"Popular place," Amy said, settling in her seat.

A server passed carrying plates heaping with French fries and sandwiches.

"It looks like they don't skimp on the servings," Gage said.

"Good, because I'm hungry. My breakfast left a lot to be desired," his mother said.

Another server stopped at their table to pass out menus. "Welcome, folks. What can I get you to drink?"

"I think it's too early to sample your alcohol," Amy responded.

Gage agreed. He didn't oppose a good drink, but nothing beat coffee. "A cup of black coffee for me. Ladies?"

"Black coffee, too," Amy said.

He liked the notion that they shared coffee in common.

His mother rolled her eyes. "Cowards. Why come to a distillery and not sample? What do you recommend?" she asked the waitress.

"Vanilla vodka and maple rye are two customer favorites. All our spirits are made from the water of six glaciers located high in the Rocky Mountains. No other place in the world is like Banff, the same goes for our spirits."

"I'm sold," his mother said with a smile. "They both sound delicious."

The server smiled. "They are. The vanilla vodka is like old style vanilla ice cream—buttery smooth and slightly sweet from the vanilla. The maple rye is sweet enough to be a liqueur."

"You've made my decision very difficult."

Gage leaned forward. "Mom, chose."

She scowled, then smiled. "Both, if you please."

He couldn't help himself and rolled his eyes. His mother could always surprise him.

"Think I'll have a hamburger," he told the two women. "Have you made up your minds?"

Amy nodded.

His mother hummed. "Well, I don't know. A liquid lunch is sounding mighty good."

Gage didn't fall for the bait. He shrugged his shoulders. "Go for it, Mom."

When their waitress returned with drinks, they placed their orders, and as he suspected, his mother ordered a chef salad.

"I read this place has tours," Amy said. "After lunch I might stay and sign up for one."

Disappointment welled in Gage's chest. "Depending on how long the tour is, we could join you."

A forced smile graced her face. "Sure, if you have time. I don't want to take you away from your wedding plans."

Her words shot an arrow into his heart. Oh hell, he didn't need a reminder of his commitment. "Trudy's handling it. She knows what she wants and doesn't take suggestions very well."

Amy's lack of enthusiasm caused him to surmise she wasn't enjoying her time with them. Not the impression his gut gave him. The quandary resolved itself because their food arrived and he inquired about the tour. Fortunately for him, they weren't conducted on Mondays.

His mother let them sample her drinks. The two spirits were delicious, as was the food. Amy insisted paying for her own meal. On the way out, they visited the retail store and his mother ordered a case of vanilla vodka and maple rye each. Thankfully, the store delivered. Amy purchased a boxed set of three sample bottles, which he offered to carry.

The stores on this side of the street were nearly identical to the ones they'd already patronized, more jewelry, outdoor clothing, or chintzy souvenir stores. It didn't seem to bother his mother or Amy. They systematically checked the merchandize in each one with equality.

At a candy store half-way down the block, his mother insisted they share a caramel apple. "Isn't this fun?" she asked, licking her fingers. "I hate for this day to end. Amy, you must have dinner with us tonight."

"I don't know…"

"Mom, she might have other plans."

Blue eyes twinkled with delight. "I'd love to…that is if Trudy won't mind."

His mother laughed. "Too bad if she does. You're my guest. We have reservations at the Italian restaurant in the hotel for 6:30 p.m."

"I'll be there with bells on."

Gage swallowed hard. He was in trouble now. The last thing he needed was to spend more time with the attractive brunette while engaged to someone else.

One thing the day had made clear to him. He was falling in love with Amy.

Chapter Six

Hard knocking rattled his hotel door as he changed for dinner. Gage shrugged into his favorite travel suede sports coat and opened the door.

A blur of crimson red brushed past him. Trudy threw herself into a chair, her dress sliding up to reveal a lot of skin. "What were you and your mother doing in Banff with Amy?"

He felt a frown turn his mouth down. "I don't know what you mean."

Trudy glowered at his response. "Don't deny it. I saw you on the corner."

"We ran into her in town. What's the big deal?"

"Nothing. Just curious. I'm looking forward to getting to know her better at the spa. We didn't associate much in college and have a lot to catch up on since leaving."

That came as a surprise. Had he made a mistake and misjudged Trudy? He stared at his fiancé and hoped she meant it. "I'm glad. I hope you have a nice time."

Trudy laughed, but no amusement lingered in the sound. "I'm sure I will."

"Mom likes her. And, if you must know, so do I. She's very down-to-earth. It's easy to relax around her, and I don't feel like I need to put on false pretenses. That's nice for a change."

Trudy leapt to stiletto encased feet and strutted before him. He inhaled strong perfume. Whatever it was reminded him of graveyard dirt. She wrapped her arms around his neck and pressed her athletic body against him.

"Kiss me," she said in a whispery breath.

He fought against the urge to push her away. Instead, he brushed his lips across her forehead.

She retreated, a look of regret flashing across her face. "Not much of a romantic, are you?"

He only smiled. "Let's go to dinner."

****

Amy spent a wonderful day in Banff with Gage and Lottie. They were fun, easy to talk with. What her grandmother called good people. When they'd arrived back at the hotel she went directly to her room.

A surprise awaited—a package from the Christmas store sat at the end of her bed. She stripped away the tissue paper to discover the tree she had admired.

Gage!

Despite the warmth spiraling through her, she knew the gift would have to be returned. Sooner, rather than later.

While fretting about how to do so without insulting him, she showered and prepared for dinner. She'd only brought one semi-dress up outfit—a pair of black wool slacks and sweater with a built-in glam necklace. She recalled wearing it once to a chiropractor's appointment and he'd requested she remove the necklace before he realigned her spine. If it could fool someone up close, surely it would work across a table.

A sense of anticipation filled her as she hurried to meet the Townsends and Trudy. The aroma of garlic greeted her as she entered the circular restaurant. She spotted a couple from the bus along the wall on the far side. They waved. She returned their greeting.

"The Townsend party," she said when the maître d' approached.

He nodded. "Right this way." He led her to a table around the corner. Gage and Trudy sat on one side with Mrs. Townsend on the other. She slipped into the open chair.

"You don't look like you spent the day shopping, Amy," Lottie said with a big smile.

"I'm like an energizer bunny. A little rest and I rebound."

"Well, you look lovely. I love your sweater."

Trudy gave her a hard stare. "It looks like a St. John. Is it?"

"Afraid I have no idea about the brand. I bought it on sale a few years ago." Amy eyed the sleek red sheath with a cutout at the shoulder that Trudy wore. It screamed high-end designer.

"What would you like to drink, Amy?" Gage asked as if to defuse an uncomfortable situation.

She didn't know what it was about his voice, but a ripple tripped down her spine, then she collected herself. "Do you have Riesling?" she asked the maître d' who had remained at the table.

"No Riesling, but our cellar offers an excellent Gewurztraminer from British Columbia."

Amy smiled. "That'll be fine."

"That's what I'm having, too," Gage said.

That tingle struck again. "A man of good taste."

"Yes, you are, darling," Trudy said, sliding her hand up his arm.

Amy read the message loud and clear. *Off limits. Do not touch.* Trudy didn't have a thing to worry about from her. She had no intention of trespassing.

Trudy lifted her glass of a blood red wine and sipped. When she lowered it, she speared Amy with a look, "Did you receive my invitation, Amy? I asked the hotel to deliver it to you and I haven't received a response yet."

"Oh, I'm sorry. I did, but with a day full of shopping I completely forgot about it. The day just flew by." Apprehension filled Amy. She hoped her explanation satisfied the other woman. Maybe she was just being silly.

A server silently placed a glass of wine in front of Amy. She smiled her thanks. They ordered their dinners.

Afterwards, Trudy leaned forward. The posture usually implied an aggressive behavior. "I know it's short notice, but what do you say? A day of rest. Most people need a vacation after going on vacation. I always treat myself to at least one day while away. Come on. It'll be more fun with a friend."

Amy suspected she was walking into the lion's den, but the expressions on Gage and his mother's faces were so encouraging, she didn't hesitate. "Sure, why not. I've got an early morning snowshoe hike to a frozen waterfall, but I should be back by 11:00 a.m."

"Wonderful. Now, onto wedding details." Trudy flashed a smile at Gage. "I've narrowed the florist down to one who can fulfil my order. There are seven churches in the general area. Since I had the time, I visited five today. St. Mary's downtown was where my parents were married. It's probably too small for our guests and parking simply was non-existent."

"I remember that day," Mrs. Townsend said. "It was my only time in Banff. Your mother made a beautiful bride."

"I think that's why my parents always took winter vacations here," Trudy said in a wistful tone. "And why it's important to them for us to be married here."

"What about the gondola?" Mrs. Townsend asked. "I hear there's a beautiful spot for wedding ceremonies at the top of the mountain."

Amy sipped her wine. The private conversation didn't involve her two cents. She'd figured out why Trudy wore the red sheath dress. The carmel-haired woman wanted to capture everyone's attention. Red was a power color, meant to intimidate. Did Trudy feel threatened by her presence? It was ridiculous.

"I'm sure you're right about the place, but I am not thrilled about it," Trudy said. "It's such a corny location. I worry about it not having the ambiance I'm looking for, but we can check it out."

"If you're worried about strangers crashing the festivities, we'll rent the whole site for the day," Gage said. "It'll be private."

Their dinners arrived and conversation dropped off.

Earlier, everyone had agreed to try the Sicilian orange insalata and no one regretted the choice. When Amy's half-order of spaghetti arrived, it was huge and delicious. She noticed that Gage ate with gusto. Trudy's selection of lasagna looked rich and cheesy, but she only picked at the dish. Mrs. Townsend had salmon and shared the same appetite as her son.

They passed on desert. A good decision.

Finished, Amy set her napkin on her plate, positive she would waddle out of the restaurant when it came time to leave. She pulled out her credit card.

"Put that away," Gage told her. "This is my treat. I invited you."

Lottie Townsend cleared her throat.

Gage chuckled. "Okay, mom, I get it. It was really your idea."

Mrs. Townsend grinned and the awkward moment passed.

Amy hadn't agreed to join them for dinner for them to pay. "Thank you. That's very kind of you."

"My pleasure."

"I'll see you at the spa tomorrow," Trudy intruded into what felt like a private moment. "Why don't we meet at 10:30? We can have a nice little chat before our appointment begins."

Amy glanced at the trio. A good meal and pleasant company was hard to beat. While she harbored no doubt that a sincere friendship could develop with Gage and Lottie, she was fully aware Trudy possessed no love for her, despite her attempt at being friendly.

****

Gage stewed as he walked his mother and Trudy to their rooms. Having dinner with Trudy and Amy only convinced him his affections for Amy were genuine. Every time he had looked at Trudy, he felt nothing. No stirrings whatsoever.

But with Amy…his pulse raced until he thought he'd pass out. It was crazy. He'd never fallen for woman this fast. This hard.

He considered his options as they went down the long hallway. He didn't have much choice. Trudy and he were going to have to sit down and have a serious chat. The idea of hurting her tore him up. They'd practically grown up together. Maybe she'd decide to call off the wedding on her own. It would be better if the idea came from her. Less hard feelings.

How the heck could he do that?

They stopped at his mother's door. "See you tomorrow," she said, swiping her key pad and slipping inside.

Trudy and he walked two doors down. She tapped the key pad and cracked open the door. "Come in and share a night cap with me."

"Not tonight."

Trudy traced his chin with her finger. "What's wrong?"

He didn't want to build up her hopes, only to crush them later. It wouldn't be fair. "Nothing. Just tired. I never realized how tiring shopping all day could be. And Mom wants to hit town early tomorrow."

She shot him a quizzical look. "Again?"

"Yep. Rain check?"

"Sure," she answered without conviction and shut the door with a soft thud.

The safety latch clicked on the other side. He headed for his own room, feeling like a heel. He was behaving like a coward.

Half-way down the hall, he spun on his heel and headed for the elevators where he went to the first floor.

Ahead, low light lit a shallow cove with burgundy leather chairs and round wooden tables. The place was empty of other hotel guests. He wondered if it was closed for the night. For a split second he almost turned around.

"Welcome, sir," greeted a familiar voice.

Gage smiled at the elderly bell-hop. "Hello, Sam. You certainly get around."

"I help where needed. Can I get you anything?"

"How about a Scotch on the rocks?"

"*Beatha na h-Alba.* An excellent choice, sir. I'll be right back."

Gage sat next to a window. Outside tall poles with lanterns lit the snow-covered ground in a magical glow. A couple strolled along a path holding hands, stopping to kiss. Sighing, he visualized himself bending over Amy and doing the same.

Sam returned in record time. He set a coaster down and placed a drink atop it. "Enjoy. Will there be anything else?"

"Only if you have a solution to female problems?" Gage said half-jokingly.

Sam scratched his white hair. "Away with ye. That's beyond my duties." He glanced around the empty room. "However, if you want to talk… Sometimes airing your troubles helps resolve matters."

"Have you ever known anyone engaged to one woman, but in love with another?"

"No, sir. I can't say I have. Never been married. Never met the right woman. You might say this grand old lady has my heart. I wouldn't want to be anywhere else in the world." Samuel swung his arm to encompass the hotel.

Gage lifted his glass, sniffed the alcohol before taking a sip. A sweet bite dragged at the back of his throat. He nodded.

"Have a nice evening, sir." Sam walked away.

A sense of relief washed over Gage. It felt good to tell someone about his predicament. He tossed the rest of his drink down his throat and savored the burn.

****

Amy rose the next morning at 6:00 a.m. to shower, dress, and head for the snowshoeing pick-up spot in the lobby. She spotted a group of six waiting near the concierge's desk, chatting with one another when she arrived. All were willing to rise early and brave the icy cold of a winter morning.

"Welcome, folks. My name is Joanie and I'll be your guide this morning. It looks like we'll have a beautiful day for our hike. Snowshoeing is the perfect activity to have fun and explore our wonderful area. This is an easy trail. Just a couple small hills to traverse. Everyone ready?"

Joanie smiled a big, toothy grin. She was a tall blonde with a hint of an accent lacing her voice.

Everyone gave her a positive reply.

Amy had rented waterproof boots, adjustable poles with snow baskets—circles around the poles to provide support and keep from sinking into deep snow—and flat terrain snowshoes.

They went outside and sat underneath outdoor heat lamps to strap on their snowshoes. Dawn cast a diffused light over the landscape. Sunrise was minutes away.

"Single-file, folks. And keep your eyes open for wildlife," Joanie said, slipping on a backpack.

"What kind of wildlife?" a heavy-set lady asked.

Joanie signaled everyone to start walking. "Lots of birds—falcons and white-tailed ptarmigans. Wolves are near the parks, but incredibly rare to see. The same goes for lynx, wolverines, and mountain lions."

"What's left?" the same woman asked.

Joanie turned around and flashed a smile. "Oh, there's plenty of deer, elk, and bighorn sheep, especially in the mornings. Keep your eyes peeled on the hills. If we see anything close, do not attempt to approach. Just remember they are wild animals."

In less than a mile, Amy's thighs burned, and she had considered herself in good physical shape. Wrong. Snowshoeing was whipping her butt. She never appreciated vigorous exercise before today.

The sun rose in all its glory and magnificent scenery of snow-covered mountains surrounded the group. They followed a tree-lined trail with a slight incline. Amy's breath came out in white puffs.

Thirty plus minutes later, Joanie held up her arm. "Quiet," she said in a low voice. She pointed to the left. "Look over by that fence."

Seven pairs of eyes turned in the direction indicated. A lone elk stood. The animal was huge. Amy never realized how big they were.

About another hour later, they reached a fifty-foot sheer hillside with a frozen waterfall of stunning blue ice. Phones came out and everyone started snapping pictures.

"You can walk behind the waterfall," Joanie announced with a twinkle in her eyes. "There's a hidden cave there. Afterwards, I've got bottled water and snacks."

"I'll go," Amy said, curious.

Up close, the waterfall creaked and popped. Her imagination went wild. She visualized a water nymph trapped in the ice until spring. She took off a glove to place her hand on the frozen mass. If she concentrated hard enough the creature's slow-beating heart thumped.

In the quiet, it dawned on her she hadn't spared a moment about Gage during the hike. But now, alone, surrounded by ice and magic, his image exploded in her head. God, he was handsome. He tempted her to break a vow of never becoming involved with a man already taken. It would only lead to heartache.

The trek back went much faster and the group arrived at the hotel just before 10:00 a.m. Amy rushed to shower and change her clothes. Even with sore muscles, she wasn't looking forward to spa day with Trudy, but maybe something good could come out of it.

Chapter Seven

Amy forced a friendly smile upon entering the spa with a minute to spare. Looking around, Trudy wasn't in sight. She set aside misgivings about her college nemesis, vowing to give the woman the benefit of the doubt.

Lavender and mint greeted her first thing. Before the door closed behind her, a middle-aged woman in a white uniform with a tiny logo of the hotel on the front pocket came through another door with a tray holding a glass of orange juice.

"Ms. Blankenship made an appointment for me and herself, but I'm early."

Smiling, the woman extended the tray. "That's all right. Welcome to the spa. Would you care for a refreshment?"

"Thank you." Amy accepted the drink.

"Ms. Blankenship just called down and said she would be delayed by five minutes."

"No problem."

"Please, take a seat and relax."

Soft music playing from ceiling speakers did its job. Amy sipped her juice and relaxed. Five minutes turned into ten, then fifteen...until the door banged open. So much for chit-chatting before their appointment.

Trudy barged inside with a wide smile, phony as hell. "Hi, Amy. Sorry to keep you waiting. Gage just wouldn't let me leave."

Envy ripped through Amy to rock her back on her heels. She took short breaths to collect herself. That statement could be taken so many ways. Then reality hit her. Was she jealous? She couldn't be, could she? Frowning to herself, she chastised herself for letting the emotion get the best of her. Then she shrugged. "No problem. I'm still unwinding from my hike to the frozen waterfall, which by the way, was breathtaking."

The same spa employee reentered the reception area with the tray and held it out for Trudy.

"What? No champagne?" she complained.

"It's freshly squeezed orange juice," Amy said, trying to divert attention from the woman being picked on. Her assistance wasn't necessary.

A frozen smile, from years of practice, remained fixed. "I'm so sorry. Your order merely requested refreshments. Nothing specific. I would be happy to provide you with something else. We want your visit at the Fairmont to be as pleasant as possible."

Trudy lifted the glass off the tray. "Don't bother. This will do. When do we start?"

"Right now, if you wish."

Amy nodded to herself. The spa employee could handle uppity patrons, and bet Princess Trudy ranked at the front of the line.

Trudy tossed down her juice and set the glass on the tray. "I'm ready right now."

"Follow me," the woman said.

She led them to a spacious room lined with cream-colored leather chairs and basins at their bottoms along three walls. They were the only patrons. The spa lady turned on water faucets at two chairs and half-filled the basins. "Remove your shoes and soak your feet for a few minutes. Someone will come and escort you to your room."

Trudy huffed and kicked off her shoes, discarding them haphazardly on the floor. "I suppose we should start. Do you still use those fish in the water for exfoliation?"

Fish? Amy stopped to hear the answer.

"No, Miss. They were considered unsafe, possibly disease carriers, so the government outlawed the practice."

"Well, I never," Trudy huffed.

Amy removed her shoes and set them alongside her chair. She sank into a cushioned seat and dipped her feet into warm water with a sigh. Disturbing the water released the hint of pine mixed with herbs or maybe eucalyptus. Both fragrances reminded her of tea tree oil. "This should be quite an experience, even without fish."

Trudy shrugged. "So, what have you been doing since you left school? You were a business major, if I remember."

"I was. But once I graduated, I found something that appealed to me more—real estate. The job requires organizational skills, understanding the housing market, communicating with people, and having the smarts to navigate the transaction. In my off-time, I even took classes in interior design. I like helping people find the right house and turn it into a home. Sounds crazy, but I love my job."

"Maybe you could help me and Gage when we decide to look for a place."

A knot squeezed Amy's heart as if a snake coiled around the organ. Not jealously this time, only empathy. She imagined how awful Gage's life would become with Trudy. Shame on her. It wasn't any of her business. "Sure. I'll give you my card. Call me any time."

She was saved from giving a sales pitch when two women—one tall and blonde, the other barely five feet with dark hair—entered the area.

"Miss Blankenship and Miss Phillips, welcome," they said in unison.

The taller blonde said, "We're your therapists. Time for your massage."

Her and Trudy's feet were patted dry and slippers placed on them. They grabbed their shoes and followed the women to a room dimly lit with two tables. Soothing music played in the background. Scented candles smelling of grapefruit burned on a windowsill.

They disrobed, then each slipped onto their stomachs on cool sheets. The dark-haired therapist stood alongside Amy's table and started by picking up her hand and rubbing her fingers, arms, and neck. The woman had magical fingers. She applied pressure using slow, deep strokes to muscles that verged on pain, but felt wonderful, especially on calves and thighs that received a workout earlier that morning.

Tension seemed to melt from her body. Amy sighed as tight muscles loosened.

If the moans coming from Trudy were any indication, she enjoyed the massage as much as Amy.

After forty-five minutes, the session ended all too soon. Amy sighed, every muscle a puddle of pudding.

"Ready for lunch. I'm starved," Trudy said while they dressed. "We have so much to catch up on."

Like what?

Amy smiled as if she agreed. "Looking forward to it."

As arranged, they headed for a hotel restaurant where they were seated immediately. Trudy ordered a glass of wine. Instinct warned Amy to keep a clear head and requested black coffee. Better safe, than sorry.

"Well, how do you like Banff?" Trudy asked.

"I'm in love with it. The scenery is drop dead gorgeous. The people are so nice. I've met quite a few Australians. And, lucky me, the exchange rate between Canada and the United States is in my favor."

Trudy gave a little snort. "Guess that's true. I did a bit of damage to Gage's hotel bill the first day. He told me to just put whatever I found on his room. I took him at his word. One shop had this super soft scarf and hat to die for. It was expensive, but I couldn't resist."

Pausing, Amy wondered if Trudy was bragging, or why she felt the need to do so. Was she insecure about being Gage's fiancé? That attitude seemed far-fetched for the confident woman. Amy shoved the idea aside when their meals arrived. For a couple minutes, she ate in silence, enjoying her food.

Trudy stuffed her mouth with a forkful of salad and swallowed, then let out a big sigh. "Being married in Banff is my parents' idea. I would have preferred somewhere warm and sunny."

Amy simply stared at her. Wouldn't a bride be more excited about getting married instead of blasé? She wondered if Trudy really wanted to get married.

With a wave of her fork as if dismissing the subject, Trudy jumped to another one. "Did you hear that Ted Roberts is getting a divorce?"

Amy's heart stopped. "Excuse me?"

A cold smile lifted lips painted bright red. "Ted Roberts. I thought you knew him. His firm purchased a couple properties through your realty office. Guess I was wrong. My bad."

Alarm bells went off. Not a coincidence. Trudy had learned of her affair and this was her mean, spiteful way of gloating. Amy hadn't known he was married when she met him, believed him when he lied about being divorced.

Gathering her resolve, she prepared for the worst. So much for the afternoon ending on a high note. This had been an ambush all along, and she fell for it—hook, line and sinker.

Hardening her spine, she steeled herself against allegations that were sure to come. "That's unfortunate. I mean...his divorce."

"His wife, Addison, is a friend of mine. She was in my sorority. He had an affair, you know, a year or so ago. Several actually. They nearly crushed her. She cried on my shoulder for days. I felt sorry for her. But the last woman... I think Ted was considering divorce. She was breaking up a happy family."

An answer was expected. "That's too bad. Betrayal can destroy a marriage."

A tremor went through Amy. She'd experienced a similar thing. Oh, sure, minor compared to his wife and family, but still painful.

Trudy narrowed those icy green eyes of hers. "Addison hired a private detective. He discovered the identity of the last woman. Addison threatened to confront her, but chickened out at that last minute. Instead, she forgave Ted. Or, tried. She worried every time he left the house that he was meeting her again. After a while, she just couldn't take the betrayal and packed up the kids and went to her parents in Michigan to file for divorce."

"I hope she finds someone who makes her happy and learns to trust again." Amy meant the words in all sincerity. She never meant for her indiscretion to cause harm or destroy a family. Now, a brick-load of guilt weighed upon her for a mistake not of her making.

****

Gage enjoyed his second trip to Banff almost as much as the first one. All the items his mother had called interesting the day before but didn't buy, she bought today with the odd explanation, 'I might as well get it now because I don't know when I'll return.'

They bobbed into a restaurant tucked into a side street for lunch to escape the bitter cold of winter. They'd ordered and awaited their meals.

For the millionth time he glanced at his wristwatch. Wearing one made him old-fashioned, but he didn't care. He wondered what his fiancé and Amy were doing. Having fun? Bonding? Or should he be worried?

He hoped Trudy played fair. She could go for the jugular.

"Stop fretting," his mother said, putting her napkin on her lap. "She'll be fine."

He sipped his coffee. This morning an article in the newspaper stated research that demonstrated that caffeine protected against oxidative stress, Alzheimer's, and dementia. "Who?"

"Amy, of course," she answered with a smile. "You're worried about how Trudy will behave."

"How can you say that?"

His mother grinned. "Because I know Trudy. And I know this engagement wasn't your idea. I'm not blind, you know. I see how reserved you are around Trudy. And the gleam in your eyes when you look at Amy when you think no one is looking."

He couldn't raise a denial. "I didn't think my attraction was obvious."

"You can't hide your feelings from me, son. I've known you all your life. I know you're agonizing over your feelings."

The conversation wasn't one he expected to hold with his mother over lunch. Not that he minded. He'd always been open with his parents. "I thought you and dad wanted me to marry Trudy, to merge the two companies."

"That's Trudy's dad aspiration. Rumor has it that he's short on capitol and knows we've always kept a high cash reserve in Cyber Technology. Even if you and Trudy wed, we'd think twice about merging the two companies."

"What a relief. I've had my own doubts about combining them. I haven't seen his financials, but planned on having a sit down with him on just that subject before the wedding."

His mother smiled. "Great minds think alike."

In the lull, his concentration drifted onto a more pleasant subject. Amy. An inner voice told him she could hold her own with his fiancé. No reason for concern existed. He smiled at the thought.

"What are you grinning at?" his mother asked.

"Just comparing apples and oranges."

"Let it go, Gage. You can't control what happens."

"Are you a mind reader?"

His mother stared at him, empathy softening the angles of her round face. "When it comes to my son's happiness, you bet I am."

"Let it go, Mom," he repeated her own words. "I can take care of myself."

"I just don't want to see you hurt."

Before he could answer, his cell phone rang. He glanced at the readout. "It's Trudy. I better take the call."

Chapter Eight

After thanking Trudy for the 'lovely experience' Amy went to her room. Trudy had brought up a painful episode in her past. Sitting on the bed, she was mad at herself. Mad at the situation. Trudy had planned a deliberate ambush, but Amy took full responsibility for her participation in the affair. As soon as she discovered the heel had been married, she dumped him. End of story.

Her self-imposed isolation lasted less than a half an hour. She stood with a jerk. Wallowing in self-pity wasn't her style. It was late afternoon. Plenty of time to enjoy the rest of the day and investigate the hotel before her nighttime sleigh ride. Supposedly, retail therapy soothed troubled thoughts. She might as well test the theory.

After meandering around for a couple hours, in one store she stroked a wheat-colored hat with a furry rabbit ball on the top. So soft, she wanted to rub it on her face. A matching scarf with tassels of rabbit fur made the perfect set. Was this the hat and scarf Trudy mentioned? For fun Amy tried it on, but after checking the price, she gulped and set it back down. It was higher than her electric bill on the coldest winter month. Too rich for her blood.

"I hope you are enjoying your stay at the Fairmont, Miss Amy," said Sam, the bell-hop when she popped out of the store. "Are you finding treasures?"

She smiled at the slight brogue—not Irish, maybe Scottish—in the bell-hop's voice. "Hi, Sam. I'm finding lots of treasures, except they cost an arm and a leg."

A chuckle caused the wrinkles on his face to deepen. "Indeed they do. Postcards are a good option and can be enjoyed over and over."

"That's a great idea. Thanks, Sam."

He nodded as though pleased his suggestion found merit. "*Dy-No-Mite*," he answered by stretching out the first syllable. "Glad to be of service. Enjoy your sleigh ride tonight. If you're in the mood, you might want to stop at the lounge and sample a hot toddy beforehand. It'll help keep the winter chill at bay. Now, I've got to be going."

Amy tried not to smile at the archaic phrase from the seventies. The bell-hop must be a fan of re-runs of the old comedy series, Good Times. Her grandmother had loved that show.

"Thank you," she said and watched the man saunter away.

Only after he was out-of-sight did she realize she hadn't mentioned the up-coming sleigh ride. How'd he know? Hotel staff gossiping about guests? Someone must have told him that she signed up for the ride. She shrugged, dismissing a little twinge.

She checked the time. Plenty left before she had to venture outside. Why not stop and treat herself to a hot toddy? She'd never tasted one before.

Decision made, she went to the bar and ordered the drink. As she waited, she glanced out the huge bay window. Night came quickly, and with it the sparkle of lights reflecting off the snow.

Her drink arrived and it was a sweet mix of whiskey, hot water, honey, cinnamon, cloves, and ginger. After a sip she couldn't believe she'd waited this long to taste her first hot toddy. Just call her an idiot.

Through the window, under the glow of lanterns, a score of people began congregating on the snow-covered lawn for the sleigh rides.

Finishing her drink, she pushed herself away from the bar and went outside. A festive atmosphere greeted her. People laughed, chatted, and smiled. No one seemed a stranger. When the crowd of merry participants formed a line on either side of the sleigh, she joined the closest end.

A voice boomed, "Four to a seat. Start with the first row."

People began to move. Amy edged forward with the flow.

Couples and families climbed aboard, alternating from both sides, and the sleigh filled. It moved away to the sound of huge bells jingling on the horses' harness. The second sleigh pulled up and the process of loading started again.

It looked like she would sit in the last row. Fine with her.

"How many?" the driver asked when her turn came.

"Just one," she said.

"There's room in the second row. Go there."

Amy dodged people already queued for the next ride. Head down, she put her foot on the step and one hand on the side to pull herself up.

"Let me help you," offered a voice that sent purls of delight undulating through her veins.

Her foot slipped. "Gage. Maybe I should take the next sleigh."

"Don't be silly. There's plenty of room," he answered. "Come on."

Embarrassment or the hot toddy burned her cheeks until it felt like her face was on fire.

He took hold of her gloved hand and pulled her up alongside him with ease. In spite of the driver's insistence that each seat held four easily, it was a tight squeeze. Heat radiated from Gage's thigh. She tried to move her leg, but it did little good.

She leaned forward. "Hi, everyone. Nice to see you here."

"Sam, the bell-hop suggested we come," Gage answered first. "It wasn't on our agenda, but I'm glad he did."

In spite of her best intentions, Amy savored Gage's greeting and nearness. She wrapped her coat tighter. It didn't produce the same comfort as the sound of his voice.

"The more, the merrier," his mother answered from the far side of the wooden seat. "How was your visit to the spa?"

Trudy glared at her. The other woman narrowed her eyes to slits.

Under the green-eyed scrutiny, Amy cringed. She didn't want her affair with a married man discussed. She wanted Gage to have a good opinion of her.

****

Already the temperature fell below freezing. The chill of the night lifted Gage's mood. New fallen snow covered the world in a pristine shawl. His bundled body stayed warm, but the surprise appearance of the petite brunette next to him delighted him in spite of noting her earlier tension.

He listened to her give an accounting of her day, mesmerized by her moving lips as she talked to his mother. He wondered how Amy's lips would taste if he kissed them.

The sleigh moved along at a slow but steady clip. Bells jingled at the movement. Pedestrians on the trail edged toward the side to let them pass.

Fifteen minutes later the sleigh pulled into a clearing and came to a stop. Horse hooves stomped the ground. They'd reached their destination far too quick for him and ended his fantasy.

"Stretch your legs, folks," their driver said, standing up.

Everyone stood at once, rocking the sleigh. Amy jumped down and set out with a wave. He heard movement behind him, but kept his gaze fixed on her as she headed away.

When he turned around he found himself alone. Trudy and his mother had disappeared as well. He glanced up at the driver still on the sleigh. "Where should I go to see the lights?"

"Look in a northerly direction for the polar lights. The display should be just over the tops of the trees."

It took only a moment for the show to begin. Gage stared unblinking for several seconds as nature put on a display of dancing green streaks lighting up the night sky. Next came glowing purple, blue, and blue Aurora borealis lights. They flickered and swayed across the blackness in a hypnotic dance.

Ohhs and aahhs erupted around him. He glanced at the enthralled specatators. He should be sharing this phenomenon with his family, so he went looking for either his mother or Trudy.

The soft whisper of voices near the tree-line caught his attention. Looking around he spotted a couple women and recognized the silhouette of Trudy and Amy. Snow silenced his footfalls and kept his presence hidden. He eavesdropped on their conversation, curious what they had to say.

"I'm sorry about this afternoon," Trudy apologized.

Gage froze with surprise at his fiancé's contrition. That was totally out of character.

Trudy continued, "I had no right to bring up Ted Roberts. I don't know what came over me. If you had an affair with him, I was wrong to mention it. It's none of my business."

Ted Roberts and Amy. He couldn't believe it. Not Amy. For years rumors persisted of Roberts being a serial cheater. That he believed. A man who couldn't honor his wedding vows wasn't trustworthy in his book. Not that he had any right to criticize. On this trip his own thoughts and actions were disloyal. He refused to conduct his life that way.

"From what you said at the spa," Amy finally said in a voice tinged with anger, "I wasn't the only one. I was as much a victim as his wife. The two-timing bastard told me he and his wife were divorced. Had been for months. He even claimed their kids weren't his, but he'd felt sorry for her."

"I feel horrible mentioning it. My parents are driving me nuts, pressuring me about marrying Gage. And the plans are driving me crazy."

"Forget it, Trudy. I understand you're under a lot of stress with the wedding."

Air froze in his lungs. Trudy had it right. It wasn't her business. Or his.

Standing in the darkness, the two women continued to talk. He snapped out of his daze to hear Amy sound strong and independent, just how he imagined.

"How are the wedding plans coming along?"

Trudy gave a nervous laugh. "We're going to the gondola tomorrow to check the location. Just hope it's not early morning. Mrs. T said they remodeled the entire structure a few years ago. I hear they leveled a gorgeous circle in the woods and snow to hold ceremonies. Attendees can sit in chairs or go to the observation deck and watch from the balcony. Afterwards, attendees are free to explore the grounds and premises. We'll see."

"I'm sure you'll find the perfect location," Amy said.

He didn't want to hear encouragement for a wedding that left him with second thoughts. It only convinced him that he and Trudy needed to sit down and have a heart-to-heart discussion.

He retraced his steps to the sleigh where the driver fed each horse an apple slice.

"Want to feed them one?" the man asked.

"Sure."

"Hold your palm flat and they'll take it with their lips."

A velvet muzzle tickled Gage's palm and he smiled. When he started to feed the next horse, someone tugged on his arm. He looked down as Amy pointed upward. "There's a red one."

"Very rare, hey," said the driver. "You're lucky to have spotted it."

Gage looked at Amy and saw another rarity. She was a gorgeous sight. One he ached to hold and never let go.

First, though, he had to resolve the delicate situation with Trudy.

****

The sleigh ride back to the Fairmont weighed on Amy. Trudy never mentioned Ted Roberts again, which suited her just fine. Maybe Trudy wasn't a troll after all, which would be nice for Gage. The instant she thought his name, he consumed every synapses in her mind. The best solution would be to stay far, far away from him… otherwise she would be lost. In love with a man already spoken for.

Taken. Taken. Taken.

Her mantra wasn't working. Not in the least. Fantasizing about him was all wrong. Tears blurred her vision. She told herself it was the cold air, but knew the truth. The knowledge of Gage being off-limits broke her heart.

Arriving at the hotel, she bid the trio farewell and marched to the reception desk. While the sleigh ride and northern lights had been a wonderful experience, she wanted to talk with someone who would be neutral.

"Is Sam on duty?" she asked a young female clerk she hadn't seen before.

Confusion crossed her face. "Who?"

"Sam, the bell-hop. He's an older man with white-hair, about five-nine. He has a slight accent. Scottish, I think."

"Just a moment, Miss." The clerk opened a door and stepped inside. The clock on the wall ticked off two minutes in slow motion before she reappeared. "I think there's been a mistake. We have no one by that name and description at the Fairmont at this time."

Butterflies erupted in Amy's stomach. A frown formed. Something wasn't right. "But, I've seen him two or three times. Spoken to him. He wears a short, red jacket with a name tag and a little pill box hat."

The young woman's eyes widened. "That style of uniform hasn't been worn in decades. My manager said the only employee ever named Sam or Samuel died in the seventies. You must have seen our resident ghost."

Cold water washed over Amy. That couldn't be right.

Chapter Nine

Amy stood at the reception desk with her mouth opening and closing like a stranded fish. Sam was a ghost. It couldn't be true. She'd talked to him. He was real.

Then she remembered Gage saying… 'Sam suggested we go on the sleigh ride tonight.' He'd seen Sam, too. They both had. That couldn't be a coincidence.

Still dazed, she turned away to head to her room. Waiting at the elevators, she didn't look when the doors opened, just stepped forward and bumped smack into Gage.

She started to jump away from his hard body as if he was on fire, but strong arms held her in place and she melted on the insides. She looked up into his grinning face. "Oh, I'm sorry. I wasn't paying attention."

"All my pleasure."

Her throat dried as she wiggled free. Now that they were alone, she wasn't sure where to start. "I was just thinking about you."

He cocked a brow, edging her away from the closing elevator doors. "Really. Tell me more."

This was her chance to talk to him without anyone else around. "Can we go somewhere to talk? I've got a couple things to discuss with you."

"The bar is still open."

She liked how he didn't hesitate for a second. "That'll work. Thanks."

He slipped his arm into hers and guided her across the lobby to the lounge. "Do you want to give me a clue?"

Shaking her head, she didn't answer, just increased her pace. An empty table near a bank of windows called to them. Sitting, Amy placed her hands on the table. Gage ordered two glasses of white wine.

"What do you know of Sam?" she began when they were alone again.

"The bell-hop?" His expression took on a curious slant. "Define know and why?"

"He's a ghost."

His dark brown eyes widened until the whites showed. *Surprise. Disbelief.* Both normal reactions. Nor did she blame him. She was having a difficult time believing it herself.

"You've got to be kidding," he said, pausing to nod his thanks as the waiter set two drinks on the table. "I've talked to him several times. He's served me drinks."

Amy took a deep breath. "After the sleigh ride, I went to the reception desk and asked for him. They never heard of the man I described. The only employee fitting his description died in the mid-seventies."

Gage leaned back and sipped his drink. "That explains a lot."

"What do you mean?"

He raked his long fingers through thick black hair. "Like I said, I've run into him several times and he always seemed to know what I was doing or ready to make suggestions. And he could disappear faster than anyone I've ever known."

A shiver wiggled her toes. Amy remembered a similar episode happening in the Castle Pantry. "He disappeared on me, too."

Gage sipped his wine, then pursed his lips before asking,

"What's next?"

"I don't know. I was hoping you might have an idea about him. He's a real ghost. I don't think I have ever met one before."

"That makes two of us. Let's say I agree with you. Meanwhile, what was the other matter? You said two things." He placed his elbows on the tabletop and leaned closer.

She blinked. His cologne teased her nose with rich notes of orange, lemon, and cedar. The pleasing scent made it difficult to concentrate. "I can't accept your gift."

"Gift?"

"Don't play dumb, Gage. It's beneath you. You bought that designer tree I was admiring at the Christmas store and sent it to me."

"A man can't send a beautiful woman a gift?"

"Not an engaged man." It crushed her to utter the words, but she meant them with her whole heart.

He set his glass down. "An honorable sentiment. I understand. I over-stepped."

He acquiesced too easily. She wasn't sure how to take his answer. Nodding, she stood abruptly. "We should probably leave."

"I'll escort you back to your room."

Dare she invite him inside?

No! He's taken. Remember?

On her floor, at her door, she fought temptation as she fumbled with the key card to tap and unlock her door.

"Good night, Gage," she said, her heart breaking knowing this would be the last time she would ever saw him again. "I'm glad I met you and your mother. You've made my trip better than you can imagine." She went to open the door.

"Amy…"

The inflection in his voice stopped her. Her cheeks burned as she turned around. Her gaze settled on his lips. One kiss wouldn't hurt. She stretched on tip-toes.

A door opened down the hall.

That saved her. At the last second she found the courage and strength to stop her rashness.

She held up her hand. "Don't say another word. Good-bye."

Rushing inside, she let the dark room wrap around her like a soothing comforter and her heart shattered into a thousand pieces. Tears stung her eyes. A deep-seated pain twisted hr insides until she wanted to curl into a ball and die. Leaning against the hard surface of the door, she drew in a shuddering breath while half-hoping to feel the rattle of a knock.

****

Gage faced Amy's door, staring at the cream barrier—solid wood—aching to break it down. A man standing in a hallway, alone, staring at a closed door must look like a fool. His world crumbled around him and he would have to do something to stop it from getting worse before it could get better.

His legs turned leaden on the trek back to his own room. Him and Trudy needed to talk. No more delays. It wasn't like him to procrastinate. Their engagement had to be called off.

In his room, he sat on the bed's edge and picked up the phone to punch in her room number. It rang and rang. No answer.

Next he tried her cell. No answer again. Maybe she was taking a shower. He tried to give her the benefit of the doubt, but his gut screamed that she was deliberately ignoring him. The icy shoulder he received on the return sleigh ride told him she'd been upset about something. Had it been so hard for her to apologize to Amy? Did Trudy spot him eavesdropping and was embarrassed?

Tomorrow. They were riding the gondola. He knew his mother would want to come along. The place held special memories in her heart. That would complicate matters, but he'd find a secluded spot for Trudy and him on the mountain top to have a long talk and end their engagement.

****

Amy caught the first bus to the Banff gondola. The ride opened at 8:00 a.m. Arriving at this time held little chance of running into Gage and his party because Trudy wasn't a morning person.

Amy wasn't the only person getting an early start. Three or four dozen people already formed a line upon her arrival. She bought a lift ticket and dashed down the steps to the bathroom before taking her place in line that wrapped around the lobby.

"Amy," Lottie Townsend voice broke through her reverie. "Amy, come join us."

Up ahead, at the front of the line, a grinning Lottie stood with Gage and a sleepy-eyed Trudy. Both Gage and Trudy looked uneasy. "No thanks. I'm fine here. They say the line moves pretty fast."

"I'm not taking no for an answer, young lady. There's plenty of room."

People turned to stare at Amy like a fool for not accepting the offer. Talk about awkward. Unwilling to cause a scene, she relented. "Oh, all right."

A loud clank announced the first gondola when it whipped around a sharp corner. They climbed abroad one at a time. Amy sat with her back to the view with Lottie. Gage and Trudy faced them.

Before the door locked, Trudy announced, "The more I think about this idea, the more I dislike it. Having the wedding at this place just doesn't appeal to me."

Amy's fear of heights agreed with Trudy, but she kept her mouth shut.

Gage's brow creased with frown lines. "It'll be okay. When we get to the top, let's talk."

The gondola ride was smoother than Amy expected. It glided up the hill. Trees ran alongside the cables. Within a hundred yards, they rose above the treetops. Lottie twisted around for a better view. Amy dreaded to do so. She kept her gaze aimed forward. A trail snaked beneath them. Two hikers with backpacks climbed the path. When they saw her looking, they waved.

Trudy huffed. "No, it's my wedding and I've made up my mind. This place is out."

"I'm not asking, Trudy. We need to talk," Gage said in a firm tone.

Lottie shifted in her seat, making the gondola sway. She faced the couple, a concerned gleam in her eyes. "Planning a wedding is stressful. Both of you should take some deep breaths."

Trudy offered a half-smile. "It's okay, Mrs. T. I know what I'm doing."

The atmosphere in the gondola thickened. Became oppressive. Amy could barely swallow. She'd been in tough situations while negotiating real estate deals, but if the princess turned into a troll and uttered something mean, she vowed to speak up.

The opportunity was taken away from her.

Gage stiffened on his seat. "I'd hoped we could do this in private, but maybe this is the perfect time to suggest we slow down. Do some hard thinking about our marriage."

Trudy sucked in a deep breath. "Forget slow. How about a hard stop? I won't be getting off at the top. I'm returning to the hotel and packing. We never would have suited, Gage. I don't care what my parents want. Marrying you was never my idea. My father pressured me. Mother begged me to cooperate, but I don't want to settle into a loveless marriage like theirs. Our wedding is off."

She stripped off her gloves and her fingers fumbled as she wrenched off her engagement ring. She slapped it into Gage's open palm.

No one spoke. Silence reigned supreme.

The gondola's speed decreased as they neared the top. Amy was tempted to leap off while it was still moving. She'd made a terrible mistake. This was a private conversation that she had no business overhearing. She should have remained firm and taken another gondola.

Gage glanced at her, then Trudy. "I couldn't agree more. We both deserve love."

Chapter Ten

"Amy, wait! I'm sorry you had to listen to my mess," Gage said as soon as they disembarked from the gondola. He had so much to say to Amy, he didn't know where to begin. "Mom, if you don't mind, I'd like to speak with her alone."

Amy stared up at him with her big blue eyes. Hints of pink shone within them. "I'm so sorry, Gage. I don't mean to be presumptuous, and I hope this isn't my fault. I'm mean…"

"Of course, you're not to blame. Trudy and I…" He paused. It wasn't his ex-fiancé's fault any more than his. "This has been coming to a head for a while. I was going to pursue a heart-to-heart with her today. I probably waited too long. I'm not making the same mistake twice. Please…come with me. We need to talk."

His mother discreetely moved off. At Amy's nod he took her hand and led her away. They found the theater empty, and sat in the first row. He faced her, taking hold of her hands.

"Amy, ever since I first saw you, there was something special about you. It wasn't just your kindness helping my mom. I wanted to get to know you, spend time with you. I couldn't help myself. I know it's crazy. Every minute away from you was agony."

She pursed her lips. Lips he wanted to kiss.

When she inhaled a deep breath, he tensed. His future lay in her hands.

"If we're going to be open and honest, Gage. I was attracted to you, too. Silly, I know. Love at first sight only happens in romance books."

"It happens in real life. Marry me, Amy. I love you and want to spend the rest of my life with you."

Blue eyes twinkled and dimples indented her cheeks. "Yes. Yes. Yes."

****

Warm and fuzzy sensations blossomed in Amy. She couldn't believe she said yes on the spot, but she did. Gage beamed at her and swept her into his arms for that long-awaited kiss. When it ended, she glanced at the doorway and saw Lottie standing under the lintel, smiling.

"Glad the two of you figured out what you wanted," the older woman said. "I think we need a drink to celebrate."

Amy stepped away from Gage to close the twelve feet to his mother. "You're not surprised about...about any of this?"

Lottie released a deep sigh. "Not with you or Gage. Only Trudy. I expected her to keep her claws in Gage a bit longer. Her father wanted the marriage and our companies to merge. Her mother and I have been friends since college. Helen Blankenship knows her husband and her daughter. She knows their faults and good points. We'll still be friends. That won't change."

Gage joined them and put an arm around each of their shoulders. "Where do we get those drinks?"

"Around the corner. Follow me."

Slipping his hand into hers, warmth and happiness melted Amy's insides. To fall in love with such a wonderful man over Christmas seemed like a magical fantasy. She must be the luckiest woman in the world.

She and Lottie sat at a table while Gage ordered two cups of coffee and a hot cocoa for his mother. It gave her a private moment to clear the air.

"You sure you're not upset?" Amy asked.

The angles of the older woman's face softened. "I have a confession to make. The moment we arrived at the hotel, I had you checked out. Amy Marie Phillips. Age twenty-nine. Oldest daughter of Carl and Nickie Phillips. Two sisters and one brother. Never married. Attended Wellesley College on an academic scholarship. Graduated with honors. Became a realtor five years ago. One of the top salespersons in her office. Decent credit rating. I'd say everything came back positive."

Amy sat, stunned. "I—I don't know what to say."

"Nothing to say, except welcome to the family."

Gage rejoined them with their drinks in hand. "Something tells me I interrupted an important conversation. Done? Everyone happy?"

"Delighted," Amy answered, then sipped her drink. Coffee was one of her favorite drinks. Whenever she had a cup her stress level dropped and her mood lifted. Nature's stimulator. "This coffee is delicious."

Gage sipped his drink. "We have coffee in common. Though nothing beats my first cup in the morning, you're right…this is fabulous."

"You get that craving from your dad. He loves coffee. I'm a hot chocolate person in the winter and lemonade in the summer," his mother added.

Amy filed the tidbit about Gage into her memory. There was so much to discover about him. And she would have years from here on out.

After finishing their drinks, he herded them to the elevator and they went to the observation deck. The icy bite of winter nipped at Amy's cheeks the moment she stepped outdoors, but joy made her so happy, she was oblivious.

They snapped pictures with their phones standing next to the giant bear created out of reflective triangles. Found a heated igloo constructed of clear plastic where people could lounge in comfort while enjoying the view on the far side. Walking around, they spotted a fifty-foot clearing perfect for weddings.

"That's what I remember," Lottie said with a wistful tone. "After Trudy's mom and dad were married, Gage's father brought me up here and took me out to the center. He got down on a knee and proposed. Of course, I had no idea what he planned at the time. Since then, I've always considered this place as one of the most romantic locations in the world."

Looking at the circle, Amy visualized a ceremony being held there. "I'd love to be married in a place like that in a white woolen gown with long sleeves. Simple and elegant. Maybe a bouquet of red roses."

Gage laughed. "Count me in. And instead of the classical wedding march, Christmas tunes can herald the bride's approach."

"I love it." She leaned into Gage. "I love Christmas. I love you."

And more importantly, he loved her. A happy-ever-after life spread out before them and she could hardly wait to take that first step.

****

Two days later, Amy sat in a limo and peered out the window one final time at the Banff Fairmont. Her dream vacation had turned into a dream life. "Oh, look! Look!"

Gage twisted in the seat. "Sam!"

The familiar figure in red jacket and pill box hat waved from the double doors of the hotel, a big grin on his face.

Amy sighed. "I wonder if we'll see him again when we return for the wedding."

Gage squeezed her hand and kissed her forehead. "I hope so. Ghost or not, I owe him a big favor for constantly pointing me in your direction."

Amy quickly pressed the button on the window. It silently glided down. She yelled, "Thank you, Sam. Merry Christmas. We'll see you next Christmas."

Author Bio

Award-winning author Darcy Carson grew up reading everything her mother brought home from the library. Reading romances became her favorite topic. Eventually her love of those novels led her to start writing them. She resides in a Seattle suburb with her husband and a prince of a poodle.

Other Titles by this author

Published by The Wild Rose Press

Dragons Return Series:

She Wakes the Night

Woman in the Woods

He Walks in Dreams

Self-Published

Beach Reads (anthology)

Magic Police Series:

Magic in the Air

A Saucy Christmas

DeeAnna Galbraith

Dedication

For Rob Hills ~ a real life friend

Chapter One

Elise Fayette had rearranged her life and accepted her fate for the next five days. She was going on a scavenger hunt for a major culinary prize.

"Your taco truck is a big success and the menu offerings for your new catering service are gold." her father had said, giving her a side hug. "Get out once in a while and make social connections. Can't stay in all the time. You need to be a solid member of the business community." He wiggled his eyebrows. "And there are actual single men out there."

She had heard this song before, but had finally caved. Not because she was man hunting or looking for community ties, but because she had a shot at the grand prize. Having her name connected with the hottest winery in Redmond and their annual gala really was a good idea. Hopefully, she'd get a partner who wanted it as much as she did.

All of which lead to her current situation. Standing in the reception area/tasting bar of Copper Circle Winery the second Monday after Thanksgiving, waiting to participate in the scavenger hunt. The winning team would combine their skills to cater the Copper Circle Christmas Gala for its wine club members. The most prestigious winery event of the season. The invitations were already out. Elise shrugged. A mini tasting presentation of her best dishes would have been so much easier.

The scavenger hunt was her cousin Joslyn Daughter's idea. Jos's family owned Copper Circle Winery and she planned the events and marketing promotions. She also considered herself a gourmet cook, although Elise had never tasted any of her plates. Elise's parents said that was because Joslyn's idea of gourmet came out of a frozen food section at the grocery store. Elise sighed. Top chef material or not, Joslyn would surely be participating on one of the teams in the hunt.

The guy standing across from Elise, Rob Culver, looked to be enjoying Jos's review of the winery's history, her family's history and the history of the annual event as much as Elise was. Which wasn't a lot, because she already knew it.

Rob's chef genius went back a half dozen Culver generations to a small four-star restaurant cozied into a two-hundred-year-old hotel on the Seine in Paris. He'd returned about six months ago from there after having spent five years learning French culinary processes. With that kind of pedigree, he could've been a real snob, but Elise didn't think so. He had a quiet, stand-offish personality. She figured his mind, like hers, strayed to his latest project in the kitchen. Rob had developed some wine-sauce blends anyone patient enough to get a reservation at his restaurant, bragged about having tasted for weeks afterward. She'd also seen pictures of his upgraded kitchen in an online post, and had a bad case of workspace-envy.

Joslyn said something, so Elise re-focused.

"We've already paired everyone. My team will be Rob Culver and myself. Then Franny Bostick and Gareth Pines. Lastly, Elise Fayette and my brother, Will.

"Each team gets the same clues and items to look for, but in a different order. That way we all aren't arriving at the same time and same place. The clues are associated with old Christmas songs, all put together by my mother. When you find the right the item, somebody will be available to write the date and time on a verification slip. We don't bring the item back because the other teams would then know exactly what to look for. Slips have to be delivered to the tasting bar before closing each night and we'll all meet here at ten o'clock each morning to see who had the best times. Then the teams will receive the next clue and item on their list. There will be points for first, second and third places. And no points if the item isn't found that day. At the end of five days, the team with the best score will win the catering service contract for the Copper Circle Winery Christmas Gala. Any questions?"

Elise suppressed yawn. Rob Culver held his hand over his mouth. Her yawn had started a chain reaction.

"Excuse me, honey, but I would like to change the team member assignments. Just a tad."

Jos's penciled-in eyebrows winged at this. The interruption came from Franny Bostick. Franny's family had arrived in the past year from Northern California by way of Texas, and purchased Sage Hill Bistro where she held the position of executive chef. Franny had taken the measure of her partner-to-be and balked. Her gaze strafed Rob and my partner, Will, and landed on Rob.

"I would like to be partnered with Mr. Rob Culver." She said his name as if she and Scarlett O'Hara had been raised side-by-side. Joslyn's words were rarely questioned, a down-turned-mouth showing this did not go down well.

This should be interesting, Elise thought.

"I think the teams are fine the way they are," Joslyn said carefully. Sage Hill was a big deal and she couldn't afford to dis the owners, who purchased a lot of their wine from Copper Circle. Elise suspected that was why Franny got invited to be a team member. She also figured she was here because her aunt and uncle owned the winery, not because she normally hung out with Joslyn and her inner circle.

Franny didn't give up easily. Her hazel eyes narrowed. "I have an idea. Just to be *fair*, why don't we put the men's names in a hat and draw for partners?"

Elise shrugged. She didn't much care who she ended up with, as long as they wanted to win as much as she did. Gareth Pines had a reputation as having a touchy personality, but was an excellent chef. She reasoned she could put up with him for a short term of five days. Will Daughter, who she knew had been to a top culinary school but didn't have much experience, stood quietly next to her.

You could almost see the wheels turning in Jos's brain, calculating a one-in-three chance would be better than just giving in and trading.

Gareth Pines frowned. He was being thrown under the bus and didn't like it. Will stayed quiet, which was his nature. And Rob Culver shifted a shoulder. At six foot and blessed with blue-green eyes and thick, sable-colored hair, he showed no cockiness at being the bone wanted by two dogs. That was refreshing.

A muscle ticked in Jos's jaw, but she walked behind the tasting bar and pulled out a piece of paper. She tore it into three strips, wrote names and folded the strips. She produced an ice bucket and dropped them in, holding out the bucket to Franny, a plastic smile in place. Franny pulled a slip. Elise came next and reached in. Joslyn made herself last.

Elise opened her slip. *Rob Culver.* She held in a smile as Jos and Franny eyed their choices and pulled in their lips in disappointment. Franny showed her slip. She was paired with her original partner and no doubt in for five days of nasty cracks or sullen silences. That left Jos teamed with her own brother. Good times.

Jos handed out the song name and clue for today. Each sheet of paper was sealed in an envelope and had Team One, Team Two or Team Three on the outside. Franny snatched an envelope, cut an openly sexual look at Rob by licking her lips, and spun without grace on the high-heeled boots she wore, mumbling, "This is ridiculous," under her breath.

Rob took the remaining envelope, labeled Team Three, then reached for Elise's jacket and held it for her. His gaze followed the other two teams as they walked away. His mouth twitched. "Dodged a bullet."

Elise slipped her arms in her coat and popped on her hat. "Thanks. Which one?"

"Mainly Joslyn. Sorry. I know she's your cousin."

"Um. We're not close. So, no judging."

Rob started laughing. "Not only because of the whole *we're a team* thing. Really not fond of the prospect of constant chatter for five days."

Elise laughed along. He was right. Joslyn loved the sound of her own voice. "Rather be in the kitchen?"

He stopped. "Versus a social situation? Pretty much every time."

She remembered he had graduated from both Le Cordon Bleu and La Cuisine Paris. Her own culinary education started with her parents and included the Culinary Institute of America. She didn't have the history or hands-on he did, but could hold her own.

"Wait," he said. "Didn't your dad have a booth at Taste of Seattle selling fish tacos in a garlic rosemary red sauce?"

"My dad?"

He nodded. "Yeah. L. P. Fayette. I never made it to the front of the line because I got shanghaied into helping out a friend at his booth, but I heard they were worth the wait."

Elise wanted to swoon and giggle in gratitude for his comment, but refrained. "Not my dad. Me."

Rob blinked. "I read the flyer. The name on the booth entry was L. P. Fayette. I'm sure of it. "Isn't your name Elise?"

She still floated on his compliment. "L'Elise Pauline, actually. Named in a fit of French genealogy. Fayette goes back to La Fayette." She smiled. "Not sure if it's the famous one or not. In any case, that was me. And I answer to Elise."

"Great name. And from what I heard, a really fine fish taco. Congratulations." He started walking again, as if he hadn't just made her week. Take that, Jos.

Elise studied their slip of paper with today's clue and item. "Thanks. Um, if I know Aunt Molly, some of the clues could have more than one meaning. I'm not big on games. How do you want to do this? We both throw in a guess and try the best guess first?"

"Sounds good to me. Mind if I drive? You can be in charge of the guesses."

Elise stopped in place. "Guy's gotta drive?"

Rob laughed. "Not really. I had the heated seats in my truck more in mind. That and leg room. If your car has both, I don't care if you drive."

OMG. A reasonable man. And his long, jeans-clad legs would be cramped in her car. "Good point," she said. "Your truck, it is."

His cab had only a chewing gum wrapper in the beverage holder. The rest showed spotless. "I mucked it out before coming," he teased. "Otherwise you'd see recipe notes and leftover herbs I usually haul around."

Elise strapped in and turned on the overhead light. "Appreciate it. I'm trying to train myself to record any inspiration that hits on my cell phone."

Rob turned on the ignition and she felt her seat start to warm. "Good idea, he said. "And easier than trying to decipher the notes I make on the fly. Literally."

She nodded. "First on our list is, *Rockin' Around the Christmas Tree*. The clue is *small, but solid*. Any ideas?"

Rob pulled his mouth to one side. "A furniture store that sells rocking chairs, or a Christmas tree lot or farm. Dozens of both around here, although I can't think how 'small but solid' fits in."

"Maybe try Granny's Furniture on West High. They have a large selection of rocking chairs," Elise said. "Or the Lee Christmas Tree Farm. It's closer."

Rob pulled in his chin. "I get the furniture store, but why that Christmas tree farm?"

"Big fat hunch," she said. "Song was recorded by Brenda Lee."

He tipped his head and stared as her. "Why do you know that?"

"Molly Daughter, Jos's mother, and my mom are sisters. They grew up loving music from the sixties. Guess that information just parked in my brain by osmosis, or whatever."

This brought on a slap to the dashboard by Rob. "I got the smartest partner. I should've guessed that after you told me that booth was yours." He stopped smiling. "Wait a minute. If Joslyn's mother made up the lists, won't she know where all the items are?"

Elise shook her head. "Nope. Besides being very clever with words, my aunt is scrupulously honest. Plus, she picked the team members to make sure the gala would be a success, whoever won."

Rob pulled onto the highway and headed for the Lee Christmas Tree Farm. At this time of year, they had only been open a week. The farm held neat rows of several types of trees and had a small barn where customers could purchase hot cider and doughnuts, or borrow a slicker if it was raining.

They walked into the barn and Elise inhaled deeply, liking the tang of the cider on the back of her tongue and the woodsy scent of cedar and pine. She made a beeline to the food table and picked up a small stack of round, flat rocks glued together and painted green to look like a Christmas tree. It held down the paper napkins put there for the doughnuts.

Rob caught up with her and grinned. "Wow. This has to be it." He turned as a man walked toward them.

"Can I help you folks?"

Elise nodded. "You wouldn't be the person who signs off on our scavenger hunt find would you?"

The man's eyes widened. "Didn't that just start this morning? Can't believe you figured it out this fast." He pulled a slip from his pocket, looked at his watch and filled in the blanks, handing it to Elise. "Good luck with the competition."

Rob took out his cell phone. "Under a half hour. Gotta be a record. I planned on being gone most of the day. Can I take you to brunch?"

Chapter Two

From the look on Elise's face, she was as surprised as he at the invitation, but Rob forged ahead. "I've been meaning to carve out some time to try a few dishes at that new place, Pillars, in Bellevue. Especially the savory raspberry coulis crepes."

She blinked a few times and nodded. "Sure. I've been there and it's really good. I mean the crepes. Lots of other dishes I haven't tried though. And um, we can strategize about the hunt."

Rob released a shallow breath. The invitation had just popped out. Simple. Not a date, really. His last date with French girlfriend, Claudine, had her melting down when he'd told her he was returning to the states to open his own restaurant. He'd ended up wearing the tarragon cream sauce meant for the roasted red fingerling potatoes. He missed Claudine, but not her high maintenance, over-the-top reactions to everything. She would shrug, call him a peasant, and strut away from any conversation not going her way. Which happened often.

Elise, on the other hand, seemed down-to-earth and straightforward. Not hard on the eyes, either. Dark, curly hair held off her pretty face with silver combs and clear blue eyes over a straight nose and pleasantly wide mouth. Was he staring? Bad form. He shook his head and turned toward the parking lot. "Strategizing. Good idea."

* * * *

Elise didn't lie. The savory raspberry coulis over the filling of his choice tasted wonderful. He called the waiter over and asked him to congratulate the chef on his behalf. Elise had been looking over the dessert menu. She smiled. "Not too many people pay their respects for all the hard work that goes on in a restaurant kitchen."

"Maybe not here. In Paris it's an everyday occurrence. I had one patron who would come into the kitchen and kiss me on both cheeks every week. After a while, he tried to get me to marry his daughter and teach her how to cook."

"You're kidding."

Rob hadn't told that story for a long time. He hadn't had the impulse, or anyone he wanted to share it with. Elise's enjoyment warmed him. "Nope."

She put down her menu. "Okay. What's our strategy?"

He hadn't had much time to think about it, but one plan occurred to him. "So far, you're the one with the good ideas. My only suggestion is that we each come up with a list of old Christmas songs and their lyrics. Picking out key words."

"That's good," Elise said. "Want to meet an hour early tomorrow and trade specifics?"

Rob stopped short of offering to meet again this evening. His sous chef was in charge at the restaurant this week, so he was free. He reminded himself again this was a game, and their partnership goal was to win the catering contract.

That didn't mean he didn't want to know more about Elise. It had been a long dry spell between dates while he set up and opened his restaurant. Her company may not end in dating, but it had proved pleasant. "Winning the hunt will give us some good exposure. Have you got any plans to use that?"

Elise laughed. "If you're that sure, maybe I should start working on that right away."

Her cell phone pinged and Elise slid it from her purse, grimacing at the ID. Rob frowned at her reaction. "Everything okay?"

She pulled up a text, scanned it and stood. "Not really. This is the second time my order for fresh vegetables for my food truck has been cancelled. By someone else."

Multiple surprises caught Rob off guard. One, he didn't realize how disappointed he'd be at their brunch being cut short. Two, *she ran a food truck?*

Elise started walking away, her focus on her phone. She mumbled, "My treat next time," over her shoulder.

Rob waved at the waitperson, threw some cash down, over tipping, and hurried after Elise. She stood just outside the door, where he nearly knocked into her. "Hey. I drove. Let me get you where you need to go. You can pick up your car, later."

She scanned the street and ran her thumb and middle finger across her forehead. "Right. Okay. Nearest Whole Foods, then an address in Redmond. I owe you one."

He started toward his truck. "On the way you can tell me about your problem."

She shook her head. "I'm beginning to think problem is too small a word."

Rob navigated downtown Bellevue traffic, heading for the freeway overpass. He risked a glance in Elise's direction. "If you don't mind sharing, maybe I could help."

She tapped in a location on her phone's screen. "This is the second time in two weeks someone stating they were me has cancelled my fresh vegetables order. And last week a junker car was parked in my truck's designated location. Then the air let out of its tires." She sighed. "I thought the first cancellation was an error, and the car thing, a prank by kids. Just bad luck, you know?"

He didn't know. It sounded to him like someone wanted to tank her business. Or at least discourage her. "Is your food truck new?"

Elise nodded. "Relatively. It's refurbished and we've only been operating a month."

"We?"

She nodded. "My partner Manny Trujillo and I. He had a taco truck in the Tri-Cities for years. When his daughter got accepted to the University of Washington, he moved the family to the north end of Seattle." We've modified our taco recipes and added spicy sliders to the menu. Building up a good lunch crowd."

They arrived at Whole Foods and found a parking spot. Elise pulled a cart. "I really appreciate this. If we hurry, we still have time to start the prep work before the truck opens at eleven-thirty."

He watched her select the best of each kind of produce needed, then paying for it in record time. They hurried to his truck, loading everything into a box in the bed. Rob really liked her efficiency and dedication to her business, her partner, and their customers. It pissed him off that she was being sabotaged. He headed for Redmond. "So, what are you going to do?"

Her smile faltered. "Besides prep these veggies in record time? First thing after lunch, get my car and talk to my produce guy to work out a way to make sure my orders don't get *accidently* cancelled. Then follow up with the towing company to see if they've found out who owns the car with all the flat tires."

Rob was impressed. She aced their first clue and if they stayed on top of it, they were on their way to winning the contest. Now, her quick thinking would probably save her food truck proceeds for the day.

He followed her directions in Redmond and they parked near a clean white van with bright red letters spelling *M & E's Tacos and Sliders ~ Best in the Northwest.* "Need help getting this produce prepped? I've done a lot of that and am pretty good."

Elise handed him a bag of tomatoes and another of butter lettuce, smiling. "Very small prep space but if we get a rhythm going with Manny, it could work. She started to tap on the truck's door with her elbow, when it was opened by a short man with salt and pepper hair and what looked like a more or less permanent smile.

"Elise! You saved our day. And you brought help." He reached for her bags and led the way inside.

Rob followed Elise and hefted his bags onto an immaculate counter in the toasty warm interior. Spicy aromas permeated the air and Rob's concentration broke for a minute, then he held out his hand. "Rob Culver."

The older man stopped working, grinned toward him, and gave his hand a quick shake. "Manny Trujillo. Unless you count the mustard and fries, there isn't much French on our menu. If you really intend to help, better wash up."

Rob laughed. He liked this guy. No nonsense and business first, but with a definite talent for cooking. He nodded and looked around to find a small efficiency sink and liquid soap being used by Elise. He stepped next to her and heard her huff out a sigh then point to a sliding glass window. "We're still late. Can you open and tell anyone out there it'll be five more minutes?" She grabbed a clean apron from a hood beside the sink and held it out.

For the next two hours he learned how a well-run food truck worked and what kind of loyal following Elise and Manny had cultivated. He enjoyed himself as they bumped hips and elbows and as far as he could tell, didn't lose a single customer.

After they cleaned thoroughly for the next day, Rob drove Elise to her car at Copper Circle. Traffic on the eastside sucked. Drive was maybe too ambitious a term for the stop and start crawl but it gave him a chance to relax. The art of the kitchen, as Rob thought of it, always made him somewhat anxious. Did his new hot-cold, or crunchy-smooth or flavor combination succeed, or would his customers look for newer and more talked-about dishes at other places? He turned to her. "Warm enough?"

She rubbed her hands together. "Yes, thanks. And thanks again for all your help. People can be finicky. Being even a few minutes late can sometimes change a customer's mind."

Rob laughed. "With you guys too?"

Elise tipped her head toward him, her eyes shining. "Their loss."

She was right and he needed to hear that every once in a while. He changed the subject. "Big turnout today."

Elise frowned. "Not really. About average. Why?"

He found it hard to imagine the two of them taking orders, cooking, and serving a crowd larger than the one the three of them took on. Rob shrugged. "Just seems like we were stretched full out. And as far as I could tell, your customers all stood there in the cold, waiting patiently."

She grinned. "That's a rarity. "And you haven't seen *Manny The Amazing* under pressure. He's run the kitchen by himself on lots of occasions. With crowds bigger than today."

"Wow. I could use a couple of him in my kitchen."

Elise shook her head. Curls that had escaped her red bandana during their stint in the truck, fell in front of her ears, but she hadn't fussed with them. Now they accented her complexion. "No chance. He enjoys being right where he is."

* * * *

They pulled into the parking lot at Copper Circle and Rob turned to her. "My sous chef's on deck this week and the Syrah here is one of her favorites. I'm going to pick one up as a thank you. Then I plan to work on our winning strategy. See you tomorrow morning at 9:00."

They got out of the truck to find Gareth Pines walking toward them, a smirk on his face. "About time you got back. We've been here an hour. Long enough to enjoy a nice Cabernet Franc. Even Joslyn and Will got back a half hour ago. Looks like we're on track to winning."

Rob cut a sideways glance at Elise. "Maybe." Her deadpan look gave away nothing and almost made him laugh out loud. She really was a good sport.

Chapter Three

Elise could hardly hold it in. She would've loved to poke a hole in Gareth's pompous-ass balloon, but since Rob hadn't jumped in, neither would she. Until tomorrow morning. She made a sad face, said good-bye to Rob, and went to her car. Unfortunately, a half dozen hours outside had left the interior really cold. She turned it on and rubbed her hands while her seats warmed.

As she started to leave, Rob appeared at the winery's glass doors carrying a wine sack. Franny Bostick came right behind him, chattering away and trying to keep up with his long strides on her tall, heeled boots. Elise wondered at the comfort level Franny experienced getting in and out of a car at various places looking for their item. She couldn't imagine Gareth letting Franny sit in the car while he checked out all the places for the both of them.

Rob smiled and waved to her as he strode toward his truck. She waved back. This earned her a less-than-gracious look from Franny, who saw the interaction. But since the Bosticks held court in an entirely different social circle, Elise didn't much care.

Her primary concern was the wrongful cancellation of her produce orders and the car that had been dumped in the licensed spot for her food truck. All of which had started about three weeks ago. Could it be a competing food truck owner? Someone who had a grudge against her, her small catering business, or was maybe unhappy with Manny? It didn't make sense. Besides, it was never a good time to deal with a problem that had no obvious basis, but her holiday catering jobs, and now, the possibility for winning the contract for the Copper Circle gala made it especially irksome.

She glanced at her digital dash clock. Four-fifteen. While driving on the eastside was never uncrowded, week day mornings and afternoons were the worst. That made her decision to go home and handle the issues about her food truck there, easier.

* * * *

Her produce provider answered on the second ring. "R and R Produce. This is Hector."

"Hi, Hector. This is Elise Fayette. We got goofed up again, today."

A slight pause followed. "I wondered about that, but it's such a busy time of the day and she sounded so rushed, I didn't question the cancellation. I'm very sorry and want to keep your business. What do you want to do about it?"

Since it was a woman Hector spoke to, that narrowed the gender anyway. "I know this sounds silly, but what if I asked for something you don't sell? Maybe heirloom tomatoes?"

Hector laughed. "Okay. Heirloom tomatoes. Will you ask for them when you're placing the order, or when you're cancelling?"

"Only if it's a real cancellation, but I'm hoping whoever is messing with us has had their fun and is done. Oh, and if you think it's a fake cancellation, can you remember to write down the number she came in on?"

"Sure. That's a good idea."

Someone spoke in the background and Elise knew Hector stayed busy all day. "Thanks for the help, Hector. Talk to you tomorrow."

That done, she called the towing company that towed the junker from her spot. They'd contacted the last owner of record for the car. He said a guy found him on Craigslist, showed up, paid cash and drove it away a couple of days before it was abandoned. He had assumed he was going to part it out, but never even transferred the title. Then the original owner had to pay for the tow. Not a happy guy.

Dead end there. Still, spending several hundred dollars on the junker and wasting time and energy playing a nasty prank, didn't ring true as just a joke. It made her nervous.

She heated some soup from her freezer and went online to find titles and lyrics of some older Christmas songs. She settled on six songs, printed them out and made notes as to how the lyrics might be used as part of a scavenger hunt. It proved to be a lot harder than her lucky guess this morning.

* * * *

Elise drove into the Copper Circle parking lot a few minutes before nine the next morning and pulled her notes together. She hadn't realized how many old Christmas songs had verses worded in a way that could be used as scavenger hunt hints. It would really be a matter of working the underlying meanings. The one hope she had was that there wouldn't be another hint about trees. Wow. The number of songs with trees in the lyrics.

She started to exit her car when Rob's truck pulled in next to her. A punctual man. Admirable. And from the thin sheaf of papers he held, he'd done the homework they'd assigned themselves. That made him downright sexy. Not that he needed help in that department.

He greeted her with a smile as they headed for the doors into the winery. "We might get a little more snow this week. To add to our challenge."

"Low and slow," she said.

He stopped on the step beside her. "That's exactly how my dad taught me to drive in the snow. Low gear, slightly slower than posted."

Elise gave a curt nod. "Then neither of us should miss any of the scavenger hunt days."

They sat in leather club chairs facing a small, circular table inlaid with copper circles. Elise shivered. The tasting room didn't usually open until ten and the heat in the high-ceilinged room was minimal. She rubbed her arms. "Not the greatest idea to meet here. Let's plan on the closest coffee shop for the next three days."

Rob took off his gloves and rubbed his hands together. "Agreed. Hey. Before we get started, did you have any luck finding your saboteur?"

She hadn't thought of the pranks being played on her business as sabotage, but Rob was right. She and Manny had lost a chunk of their forecasted income the day the mystery car was abandoned in their spot, and the first time their product order was cancelled. "No luck with the abandoned junker. But I did work out a sort of code with my produce guy so the fake cancellation doesn't happen again."

"Good idea. Now you have to hope no one fakes food poisoning. Or like when people brought a silverfish in a small jar and let it loose on their salad so they'd be offered a free meal to keep them from spreading the word."

"Enough," she begged. "I don't need that thought running through my head."

"Sorry. You're right. We need to get the jump on these clues. I want us to win."

Elise nodded. He didn't know how badly she wanted it and had planned to work hard no matter which partner she was assigned. "Me too." She spread out her papers. "I listed the most popular older Christmas songs played on YouTube, then key words in the lyrics. I tried to avoid some of the most common words, like tree . . ."

Rob chimed in ". . . or snow or bells."

"Yeah, but they can't be ruled out." She sighed. "How about we trade our homework and see what our partner came up with?"

Rob held out his papers. "I didn't think of YouTube. I googled the ten most popular Christmas songs for each of the years nineteen forty through the end of nineteen fifty-nine."

"I think we're covered then," she said. "Although knowing my Aunt Molly, there has to be at least one song we haven't considered."

"At least. It occurred to me on the way over she might stick in a Christmas song in a foreign language. Like *O Tannenbaum* in German, or *Feliz Navidad* in Spanish."

Elise bobbed her head. "Sneaky. And just like her. Good going, partner. We'll add those."

* * * *

Rob liked his partner. She had smarts, an easygoing personality, worked hard, looked low maintenance and still appeared pretty. Oh yeah, and she smelled great, without overpowering him. All nice attributes he appreciated.

They finished reading each other's pages at about the same time. Rob set her pages on the table. "I think we have a running head start. Yesterday's win was based on the girl who sang the song. Do you want to add those names into the mix? Kinda hard to do as they've all been recorded by so many singers over the years and even instrumental."

Elise picked up her pages. "We could take a stab at some of the most popular. Like Bing Crosby singing "White Christmas.""

Although it would be hard to come up with a clue based on the words Bing or Crosby."

He laughed. "If I come up with the best names, will you share your recipe for that red sauce you put on your tacos?"

She arched an eyebrow. "I bet if you tried really hard, you being a chef who specializes in sauces and all, you could deconstruct it and come up with something even better."

Rob pulled his mouth to one side. She was probably right, but he realized that wasn't his goal. When he'd said share, he realized he'd meant to spend more time with Elise. "Not the point. Your sauce undoubtedly needs *your* special touch."

Her frowned question, *What the heck does that mean?* changed in an instant. She smiled and stood. "Aunt Molly."

Rob turned to seeing a striking woman with dark curls similar to Elise's, only sprinkled with silver, walking through the winery doors. "Hey, you two. I see you put the other teams to shame. At least in round one."

He and Elise said 'best partner,' at the same time, then both laughed.

Molly Daughter joined in. "Well then that explains it."

"Explains what?" Joslyn asked, standing in the doorway, removing her Cashmere scarf.

Molly faced her daughter. "Nothing important. We were just discussing the first day of the hunt."

"Oh. Were they explaining how awful their time was?"

Molly Daughter swiveled her head so only he and Elise could see and winked. "An assumption on your part, Jos. The numbers say something different."

Rob liked Elise's aunt. She seemed more grounded and friendly than her daughter.

"Since Jos is on one of the teams, I need to get the envelopes ready to hand out for day two," Molly said, walking into the small office behind the tasting bar.

Jos wandered over and craned to see the papers spread on the table between Elise and him. "What's this?"

We picked up our pages and folded them in half. "Just immersing ourselves in the game," Rob said.

Jos smirked. "Didn't help you much yesterday."

Rob liked that neither he or Elise responded to being baited. He didn't know about her, but he'd learned in French kitchens the best chefs let their dishes speak for them.

In the next few minutes, the rest of the team members arrived and Molly Daughter came out from the office. "Welcome, teams. Yesterday's times were about as expected, with the exception of Team Three. They found their item in twenty-seven minutes compared to the six-plus hours of second place and nearly seven hours of third place. That being said, Team Three, Rob Culver and Elise Fayette have three points, Team One, Gareth Pines and Franny Bostick have two points, and Team Two, Will and Joslyn Daughter have one point."

She was barely finished when Gareth Pines spoke. "There has to be some mistake or they got a really easy song and clue. Twenty-seven minutes is not believable."

Molly Daughter sighed. "It could be luck or smarts or a combination. If you remember the rules, the times were to be reported by the close of the winery the same day. The fact that they chose to bring in their signed off slip after the other two teams was well within that time. I have also verified the results with the people who have agreed to validate each team's findings. Their time is correct. And, Mr. Pines, you can determine the difficulty of the clue yourself. I have assigned you and your partner the clue Team Three worked yesterday and vice versa. Good luck."

Chapter Four

Rob held back a smile. He didn't consider himself a fan of the other chef. Not because Pines wasn't good. He was. But word got around and was backed-up by more than one person who had worked in Gareth's kitchen that he berated and generally mistreated his staff. Now he was practically calling him and Elise liars or cheaters. From the sour look on Franny Bostick's face, she agreed with him. Well, as Molly had said, good luck to them. He didn't think there was any way they could beat his and Elise's time, but he was almost certain he and Elise could beat theirs.

On the way to the parking lot, Elise touched his arm, stopping him. "Your truck has the leg room you need but my compact has better gas mileage. If you end up driving all over the county for five days, I insist on helping pay for your gas."

Rob started laughing.

Elise held her pages with one hand and fisted her fluffy pink-mittened other hand on her hip and frowned. "Why is that funny?"

He stuck out his hand to shake. "Because you aren't concerned about us winning the scavenger hunt, you're concerned about being fair by paying your way."

She shook his hand and shrugged, a mischievous grin in place. "Gotta admit, when I heard the times the other two teams turned in, I more or less figured we have it in the bag. So, yeah, if you're concerned, let's give it today and then we can call it in for the last three days."

Still smiling, Rob turned toward his truck and unlocked it with his key fob. "Great attitude, but don't start planning the menu for the gala before we see what took Pines and Bostick over six hours to solve."

Elise climbed in the cab and fastened her seatbelt. Rob got in and handed her the envelope. She left it on her lap and turned to him. "Did you get the feeling Aunt Molly is rooting for us to win?"

Rob thought for a minute. "I know she's part owner of Copper Circle and more than half of each ticket sold will go to a food charity. That's the reason, besides the contract, that I rearranged my schedule to be here. It's only natural your aunt wants the best team to get the contract. Is that what you mean?"

She tipped her head a couple of times. "Will has the education, but not the experience. Jos would let him do all the work while she pushed the wine. Not the combination Aunt Molly, even though she's their mother, is looking for to sell tickets. Gareth Pines has got talent and experience but would probably be looking for self-aggrandizement. As far as I know,

Franny hasn't any kitchen experience and was invited by Jos because of the strong ties between Sage Hill and Copper Circle. Another weak partnership. Based on all that, you're probably right."

He shook his head. "Didn't know most of that. Except for the part about Pines." He pointed to the envelope. "Then let's not disappoint Aunt Molly."

She tore it open. "Or ourselves."

"The song title is "Silver Bells." The clue is white socks."

They stared at the paper for a minute. "At least a couple of feasible options for silver bells float to the surface," Elise said. "White socks is a mystery, though. Socks that hang over the mantel? White socks that are part of a holiday outfit? Yikes."

Rob huffed a breath. "We both had the song on our lists, but neither had the word socks as a clue. Let's list some combinations. What did you have in mind for the couple of options for silver bells?"

"The first is silver handbells. You know, played by groups or teams or whatever, usually during the holidays. Maybe there's a group that wears white socks as part of their ensemble costumes."

Rob started nodding. "That's good. Easy to check I would think. What's the second?"

Elise's turn to sigh. "Another total long shot. I have a friend who rides horseback with a group at the holidays around the back roads of Carnation. They decorate their horse's manes with silver bells that ring as they ride. How white socks works with that scenario is beyond me. It's usually so cold they're all bundled up."

He started the truck to warm the seats and cab. "Can you google any handbell groups nearby we could contact?"

She was bent over her cell phone. "Way ahead of you, but my fingers will work better out of my gloves." She pulled them off.

Perfect opportunity, Rob thought, and reached for her hands, holding them between his and rubbing lightly. "That better?"

Elise cut him clearly confused look. "Are you flirting?"

Blunt, but she'd caught him and he was embarrassed. "Oh, sorry. Just trying to get my partner's fingers working faster."

Pink flags appeared on Elise's cheeks. "Um, in that case, thanks."

* * * *

She felt a blush warm her cheeks. Why had she said something so stupid? Why on earth would a handsome, talented, and well-established man like Rob Culver flirt with her on the second day after they'd met? She looked at her fuzzy gloves, hooded barn jacket, jeans, and faux-fur lined boots. Nope. No glamour here. However, she knew next to nothing about Rob's private life. Maybe he thought nothing of flirting and hoping for a conquest of anyone in a skirt. Scratch that. Anyone with female parts. Or maybe he was telling the truth and she had just embarrassed them both.

Concentrating on her cell phone, Elise googled *handbell groups near me*, and smiled. Not a request googled too often. She got two hits. The first group was at a local junior college and went by The Ring Ring Rings. The second group billed themselves as professionals and were named Clarity. She called the first number and put it on speaker. *Eastside Junior College. We are closed for winter break and will resume classes on January third.* She scrunched her nose and ended the call.

Rob shrugged. "Good news. We get to eliminate one right off the bat and that ups our chances for the second one."

She liked his positive attitude. "Okay. Second call." When answered, handbells played the first eight or ten notes of "We Wish you a Merry Christmas." Then a recorded voice announced, *Hi, this is Tuesday, December eighth. We will be practicing at Meydenbauer Center from ten until two. Please purchase tickets to our concert here on December twenty-first. Thank you. Leave a number and message at the tone.*

"They probably won't pick up calls until after practice," she said. Want to just show and hope we can take a minute of their time?"

Rob put his truck into gear. "Agreed. This time of day we should be there in a half hour."

Almost thirty minutes exactly had them pulling into the Meydenbauer Center parking garage. Inside, several of the perimeter rooms were closed, but they could hear Jingle Bells being played in the large, center room. Elise looked at Rob and they both smiled as she eased open one of the access doors. On a tiered platform, she was surprised to see about a dozen people in street clothes standing in front of a long table with bells of all sizes and elevated music stands. They were finishing the last chorus of the song. It sounded so cheerful she wanted to dance over to the man with his back to them, conducting, but quashed the impulse.

Someone hit a wrong note and Elise winced. Then she looked behind her and saw why. Rob stood smiling, hands in his jacket pockets, and several of the twenty-something girls were gawking at him instead of paying attention.

The conductor tapped his music stand and turned, frowning. "You're interrupting. No one is allowed in here during rehearsal."

Elise decided these were probably not the silver bells they were looking for, but had to take them off the list. "I'm so sorry, but we're playing a scavenger hunt game with Christmas song titles and hoping your silver bells would be the clue we need."

A vein throbbed in his temple. "I'm afraid not, young lady. And you should be ashamed of yourselves."

Rob stepped forward. "We forgot to mention the scavenger hunt is for charity."

This flustered the conductor and his gaze slid to his handbell musicians. "Oh, well, in that case, you are excused."

Saved by her partner, Elise tipped her head. "Thank you."

In Rob's truck, she sighed. "Well, that blew an hour. But it needed to be checked out."

He nodded. "Can you give your friend the horseback rider a call to see if we're even in the ballpark? See if white socks rings any bells, no pun intended?"

She pulled out her phone, scrolled through and touched a listing, activating a call. "Good idea. Save us some time."

Her call went to voicemail. "Hi, Meghan. Can you get back to me regarding your annual Christmas ride as soon as possible?

And let me know if the term white socks is related to it? Thanks, Elise."

She turned to Rob. "What next? We can find a coffee shop in or near Carnation or between there and Redmond and wait for Meghan's call while we go over more possibilities."

"Sure," he said. "Have you heard from Manny today? Is everything okay at your food truck?"

Nice of him to ask, she thought, since her own mind had been focused on the scavenger hunt all morning. "Nope. Which is a good sign. He lets me know right away if there are any bumps. Besides, his daughter helps him out on Tuesdays and Thursdays so it's a little easier to handle."

He smiled. "Great. I really like your partner."

And she was beginning to really like *this* partner. But said nothing, and scanned both sets of pages while Rob drove. He found a little independent coffee shop in the Union Hill area and they settled in.

Elise sipped her gourmet coffee and swooned. "This is really great coffee. Has some oomph or grabs hold and tastes good doing it. Next time I have truck duty, I'm driving over here to caffeine-up."

Rob laughed and winked at her.

"Oh, no you don't," she said. "Instead of laughing at my passion, put your brain to work and solve today's clue."

Chapter Five

Rob wished she hadn't said coffee was her passion. Or that instead, she had associated the word with him. Her dark blue eyes sparkled and those curls had escaped again. He wondered what those silky, springy curls would feel like in his hands, then forced himself to concentrate. She was right. She had come up with yesterday's winner and both suggestions for today's clue. His only contribution had been as driver. Well, and as food truck window guy. Which wasn't a real big help.

Silver bells and white socks. Silver bells and white socks. He sipped his own coffee. Elise was right. The coffee here was great. When they won the contract, part of the catering for the gala could be a coffee bar. With this shop as the supplier.

Focus, Culver.

She stared at him.

"What?"

"I hear the cogs, but nothing is being produced."

He looked over her shoulder. "Hoping the coffee would help, but all I got is way out in left field."

"Like?"

"Like maybe they aren't real silver bells, but a store window display of pictures of bells. A store that sells white socks."

Her look remained sober. At least she didn't laugh outright. "Or," she prompted.

Sweat gathered at his hairline. She was really making him work. "Thinking on the fly, here. But how about a boxing gym? You know. The silver bell that times the rounds and at least one of the boxers is wearing white socks."

Elise didn't blink for what seemed like a long time. "Um, not very Christmasy. But inventive. You get points for thinking outside the box."

"I believe it's called a ring," he said.

She popped a grin. "I'm trying to imagine Aunt Molly sitting in her tidy office and coming up with that scenario. Much less Gareth and Franny." She held up her fist for a bump. "And that is why we are going to win."

He tried to keep up and failed. "Because I thought of weird stuff?"

"Exactly. We're throwing everything we have at it. No matter how ridiculous. Gareth probably knows Meghan, too, but even if the horse and socks things isn't the clue, we're way ahead." She looked at her cell phone that sat on the table between them. "We're out only a little over an hour. I bet we crush their time."

Rob's eyebrows bobbed. "A lot to live up to."

"We can do it," she said, then jumped when her phone rang. She put it on speaker.

"Who was the snobby redhead with Gareth?"

Elise laughed. "Hi, Meghan. Thanks for the call back. That was Franny Bostick. New executive chef at Sage Hill. Why snobby?"

"She acted like she was standing in a steaming pile of horse pucky the entire time they were here. Gareth wasn't much nicer. I hope you were luckier. Partnerwise."

"Very lucky. I'm partnered with Rob Culver."

"Yum."

"He's ah, sitting right here and you're on speaker."

"Oops."

"That's okay. Something I can hold over your *married* head. Down to business. Since you've admitted Gareth was there yesterday, are you the clue we're looking for? If so, what the heck do white socks have to do with silver bells?"

"Rules say you have to be present to be signed off. Can't call it in. But speaking of married, my husband always rides his horse, Baron, in our Christmas parade. Baron has three of them."

"Got it. Learned something new, and we're on our way."

"Yay. That means I have the afternoon to take the kids and run errands. See you."

Elise reached and gently brought his chin up to close his mouth with her index finger. "I'd say great minds think alike, but Gareth was," she checked the time, "about four and a half hours behind on his brilliance."

Rob warmed to her touch. Silently agreeing her guess was lucky, but brilliant, and happy to be sitting with her in this cozy coffee shop. He slid deeper into his chair.

Elise popped up. "Don't get comfortable. We need to get to Carnation, have our find signed off, and . . ." She held out her hands. "Up to you. Once we have it, we're free to deliver it to Aunt Molly right away, or take it to her before closing."

He nodded. "Is there anything in the rules about hanging around the winery and harassing the other two teams when they come dragging in hours after us?"

A look of mock horror crossed her face. "Um, not in writing. I'm sure taking the high moral ground will suffice."

She made him laugh. Something that had been missing in his life since he'd returned to open his own place. "Spoil sport. I need to go by the restaurant to see how my second-in-command's coup attempt is working for her. How about meeting me for a flight of wine at Copper Circle, around eight? We can turn in our time then."

Elise flattened her lips and stared through the tops of her eyes. "Sounds like a good plan, but we have to get that slip first. Up, driver. Daylight's burning."

Rob laughed. "Been watching John Wayne movies?"

"The Duke is one of my grandmother's favorites," she said. "You could learn."

* * * *

Meghan was ready for them. She had the paper filled out and added the time when they arrived. They walked to the barn and saw Baron with his white socks. "Your Aunt Molly is truly sneaky. She knows that at least one person on each team is familiar with the Christmas ride. You guys figured it out a lot sooner than Gareth and the snobby redhead, though."

Meghan winged an eyebrow at Rob. "Brains *and* pretty blue-green eyes."

Rob pointed both index fingers at Elise. "She's got the brains and pretty eyes."

Elise took a second to smile at him for the compliment then picked up Meghan's left wrist and flapped the hand with the large diamond set at Rob.

"Okay. I'm happily married, not dead," Meghan said.

"I attended the ceremony." Elise responded. "But right now, we all have other errands."

Meghan picked up a toddler, bounced him on her hip, and sighed. 'Yes, we do. See you two at the gala."

Elise nodded, chucked the little boy under the chin and put the paper slip in her pocket. She reveled in the nice thing Rob had said about her, but shrank a bit at the sly look Meghan tossed her when he turned toward the driveway.

In the cab, she pulled out the slip and shimmied in her seat. "Just under two hours."

Rob smacked the heel of his hand on his steering wheel. "No kidding. One more day like this and we should be uncatchable." He grabbed her hand and squeezed it. "All due to you."

Elise wanted to pull her hand away, and at the same time, squeeze his back. His touch galvanized her. What was going on? She chose to take it back under the pretense that she needed to straighten their papers. Her cell phone rang.

Saved. It was Manny. She glanced at the clock on the truck's dash. He'd never called her in the middle of the lunch crush. "Hello.

"He's gone now," Manny said, his voice tense.

Elise frowned. "Who's gone? Are you and Angel okay?"

"We're fine. Can you drop by? I know you're in the middle of that scavenger hunt and it's important, but this old guy has me rattled."

She put her hand over the speaker. "I need to get to the truck right away. Something's happened."

Rob nodded, starting the ignition. "Twenty minutes. Is everyone okay?"

"We're on our way. Be there in about twenty minutes." She ended the call and turned to Rob. "I don't know the details, but Manny said something about an older man rattling him and he wanted to talk to me."

True to his estimate, Rob pulled in close to noon. "I can help out in the truck while you talk to Manny."

Elise already had her hand on the door handle. "Oh." She looked at the crowd standing in line. "Whatever upset Manny, doesn't seem to have affected business. But, thanks. That would be great."

They approached and opened the door. "Rob has offered to man the window while Angel fills orders, Manny. So you and I can talk. Okay?"

Elise's partner nodded and stepped down, passing Rob.

She rubbed her hands together. "Smells like snow."

Manny tipped his head. "About this old guy."

She was twenty-eight and Manny about a dozen years older, so an 'old guy' must have been in his sixties or so. "Did he threaten you or Angel?"

"Worse. That I could've handled. He came to the window waving a piece of paper yelling we'd given him food poisoning yesterday. He had a bill from the emergency room for having his stomach pumped and he almost died. He was going to sue and get the county inspector out here to shut us down."

High on the list of nightmares for people who served food to the public. She should have known whoever was jacking them around wasn't done.

"Did you recognize him? Had he been to the truck before?"

"I think so. I remember wondering why a guy who looked retirement age came to a food truck to get lunch with all the young techies in the area." He waved an arm at the buildings on the block. "As far as I know, these are all tech-related businesses."

Elise turned to walk back. The rest of the people in line watched them. Except for the women, of course. Rob stood at the take-out window. She refocused on Manny. "Why did he leave? Did he say?"

"He said he would come back tomorrow with his attorney and we should be prepared to pay his out-of-pocket of $1,100."

"Damn. Did you agree?"

Manny pulled up his shoulders, affronted. "Of course not. I don't think we should."

Elise agreed but wanted to know the impact of the scene the older man made. "Did a lot of customers leave?"

Manny almost smiled at this. "Not really. Maybe one or two. The rest just stood back and let him rant. Didn't want to lose their place in line."

That made her smile. Thirty-two degrees out, a couple of indoor eateries within walking distance, and Christmas shopping online available. Yet, here were the faithful, standing and waiting quietly for their turn at the window. "Did he say what made him sick?"

"No. Just yelled about his bill and said he'd be back. Do you think we should consult an attorney?"

"Not yet. I have some questions for our complainer. I'll be here tomorrow when we open."

Manny nodded. "Thanks."

Rob and Manny traded places and Rob brought two drinks and four tacos with her special red sauce. "Let's go heat up the truck. It smells like snow out here."

Elise was surprised. Guys as tidy as Rob usually didn't like people eating in their trucks. "Are you sure?"

He nodded. "I keep a large roll of plastic in the bed. Serves to keep market produce and other foods I pick up fresher. It'll be like a picnic."

She got in the cab and he handed her the food and drinks then took out a three-foot wide roll of plastic and cut off a piece with his knife. Elise rolled her eyes and pulled in her lips as he covered their laps and tucked a corner into the V of his jacket. He took a large wad of paper napkins from his pocket. "I can be messy."

The tension of her situation slid away as she burst out laughing.

"First these great tacos. Which I did pay for, by the way. Then we tackle this heckler and what to do about him."

Elise shrugged. If Rob wanted to insert himself into her and Manny's problem, she could always use another opinion. "As long as you remember we have another goal. To win the contract for the gala."

Rob leaned forward so as not to spill. "We can do both." He closed his eyes and hummed. "These are amazing. You should bottle this sauce."

"I've had an offer."

He finished his bite. "Really? To bottle it? That's great. Who from?"

Elise shifted a shoulder. "They're not national, but a pretty big deal locally. Their bottling plant is very high tech. My concern is my flavor won't translate into the size of batches they want to produce."

"Yeah. Sometimes a pinch of a spice doesn't work nearly as well when added as a cup."

"I need to make up my mind, soon. It's between me and another local talent. I have first option to sign or decline."

"Who's the other guy?"

"How do you know it's a guy?"

He bowed from the waist awkwardly, and clicked his heels together. "Let me rephrase. Do you know who your competitor is?"

Elise shook her head. "Not a clue. The manufacturers stated it was in case we decided to form a partnership and hold them up for more money."

"Not a trusting bunch."

She shrugged. "No. Only one of the reasons I might pass on the offer. I kinda like my niche with Manny."

His brows knit together. "Then why are you so set on winning the catering contract for the gala?"

"As happy as I am with my food truck partnership, my small catering business really needs exposure. So that's what I'm after. Exposing myself."

Chapter Five

The instant the words left her mouth, Elise cringed. "Um. I meant to say exposing everything my catering service has to offer." She couldn't meet his gaze. "What about you? Your restaurant is a huge success. Don't tell me you're going into the catering business."

Rob leaned down to catch her look, grinning. "Leaving my sous chef in charge of the haute cuisine and opening a new, smaller restaurant with basic French country food staples like *poulet roti* and French apple cake. Without exposing myself."

Elise chose not to take the bait and embarrass herself further. She also wanted to hear more about his plan. "No kidding. That sounds great. When will you open?"

"Signed a lease for a space at the square. I hope to open on the first business day of the new year."

She was astonished. Six weeks to the opening of a brand-new restaurant and he still took the time to help her out.

Yesterday *and* today. She gave him the two-finger wave-over. "In that case, I appreciate your help all the more."

Rob leaned in and presented his cheek, the plastic sheeting crackling loud.

Elise realized she meant to convey gratitude, but her gesture might be misconstrued since she'd accused him of flirting just yesterday. So she added, "You're a very nice man."

He wiped a smear of red sauce from the corner of his mouth and moved back into his seat. "Thank you."

Damn those blue-green eyes. She fumbled with her cell phone, checking the time. "Getting late if you plan to sneak up on your sous chef."

Rob pulled everything into a plastic ball, got out of the truck and threw it in a nearby trash.

When he got back in, he turned to her. "What's your plan for tomorrow?"

She didn't think he was being nosy. He had a right to know. "I told Manny I'd be here at eleven when that guy said he would show up with his attorney. I guess depending on tomorrow's song and clue we could work it for an hour then you could drop me off here and continue."

He lifted an eyebrow. "Seriously? Today's time will probably net us first or second place. That's due to you. Secondly, no one messes with my partner and my man Manny, and gets away with it. Not happening."

His little speech gave her a warm fuzzy. "Okay. What's your solution?"

"I doubt if we'll beat yesterday's time, but I'm sure we can spare fifteen minutes to set a guy straight about what he can and can't get away with. I saw the prep areas and quality of produce used yesterday. No way."

Rob was right. The claim of being poisoned from food prepared in their truck was ludicrous. It had to be an attempt to scare away customers or scam them for money. She didn't like confrontation but wouldn't back down from the guy's claims. "I guess we can spare fifteen minutes. Thanks again."

They drove to Copper Circle and turned in their documented find. Molly Daughter scanned the paper and gave them a big smile. "Good work."

* * * *

The snow they'd felt in the air yesterday skim-coated the area with about an inch overnight. Rob stored a couple of hay bales behind his garage to give extra weight to the bed of his truck for balance. He pulled onto I-90 and gave a wide berth to cars driving too fast or way too slow. He hoped the distraction of concentrating on safety would pull him away from thoughts of Elise. Three more days would end his time with her. Good news, bad news. He wanted more time to see if the feelings tugging at him were about genuine interest or just lust. He grinned. Right now, lust was winning.

Rob dodged a soft-top convertible with a woman driving in the center lane. She was going about twenty and he could see through the driver window she had a death grip on the wheel. If an inch of snow resulted in that kind of reaction, she was an accident waiting to happen.

The parking lot at Copper Circle held two other cars. One belonged to Elise. That made him happy. He scooped up the cardboard container with two coffees and headed inside.

Elise stood sideways to him, warming her hands at the circular gas firepit rimmed in copper. Molly Daughter stood at the tasting bar, going over paperwork. Both women looked up and smiled. Rob nodded at Molly and held the container toward Elise. "Coffee, partner?"

She wore a wide, dark blue band that held her hair away from her face and covered her ears. The color complemented her eyes. She pulled it down and turned her head toward her aunt. "Told you he was a nice man."

Rob kept his smile in place. "Nice man," could be applied to a bus driver who made sure he was close enough to the curb for departing passengers. Is that all she thought of him? And why did he want more?

Elise handed him their cheat sheets from yesterday and sipped her coffee. "Any guesses for today?"

He shook his head. "Way too many options."

She looked around the room. "Afraid I spent a lot of time worrying about confronting that guy this morning. Sorry."

"Thought about it some myself. This harassment might be related to the other attempts to disrupt your business."

Elise winced. "Yeah. On one hand, we could try and associate him with them and learn who and why. On the other, if he's a single incident and successful in proving it, our insurance would take the hit and we could end up with higher premiums plus lose some customers."

"Not going to let that happen. I was there, remember? I wasn't counting, but at least four dozen tacos were sold. I'm sure Manny has the exact amount. In any case, not another person has come forward to claim they got poisoned, or even that the food tasted off. Nope. It's a bluff and we're going to out him today."

She blinked. "Okay, then. Am I allowed to take notes and applaud afterward?"

His mind shot to an entirely different kind of win and he took a step back from the firepit, having warmed at the thought. He smiled. "Not necessary. I've had a couple of experiences with upset diners I can draw from."

Jos and Will Daughter came through the doors. "You drive like a grandfather," she accused.

"Then drive yourself next time."

"Or drive a macho truck," Gareth Pines said, walking in behind them and picking up the conversation.

Elise stepped toward Rob and whispered, "What's *his* problem?"

He shrugged. "General crankiness. Or it could have to do with how long it took them to solve puzzle number two."

"Maybe. We turned in a good time, but Joslyn rides a lot. He knows Meghan through her husband but I have no idea how much he or Franny knows about horses. If anything at all."

Molly Daughter consulted the slips in front of her. "Yesterday's points are as follows. Team two, three points, team three, two points, and team one, one point. The race is on, with no clear leader, yet, and two of these clues have already been found by other teams. Congratulations to all of you." She held out the envelopes. "Day three, and good luck."

They walked to his truck and Rob opened her door, then got in, turned on the heat, and rubbed his hands together. "Two points. I'm okay with that. We still have a slim lead. What's the next hurdle?"

Elise tore into the envelope. "I am, too. Let's see. 'Winter Wonderland' is the song. Pointing north is the clue."

It was light outside, but Rob flipped on the overhead cab light and Elise handed him his sheets. "Looks like we both have the song, and for clues, sleigh bells, birds or bluebirds, meadows, snowmen, and parsons."

He frowned. "So, do we eliminate the obvious ones and work from there?"

She huffed a breath. "Sure. Points north, points north. What points north? Um, not sleigh bells. Birds could fly north, or any other direction for that matter."

"There's North Meadows Park in Bellevue," he said.

"Oh, that's good. What else? Parsons can point north. Is there a statue of a religious sort in the park?"

Rob shook his head. "Not that I recall. Just the standard baseball and soccer fields plus a lot of flowers and greenery."

"Okay. Let's table parsons, but hold onto the park. How about snowmen? It snowed last night, so someone could have built a snowman there. With stick arms. One pointing north."

"True," he said. "But another team has already scored with this song and clue and there hasn't been snow."

"Drats. Pokes a hole in that theory."

He grinned. "Drats?"

She crooked that pretty dark eyebrow. "Yes, drats. An expression of annoyance or irritation."

He held up his hands. "Clean language. Another plus."

"What's that mean?"

"It means I was right the first day when I said I won the partner lottery."

"Oh. Well, thanks." Her gaze moved to her watch. "We should get moving. I want to be at the truck before it opens. To check out this guy."

Rob handed her his cheat sheets. "We made good headway. Once we handle this faker, we can go to the park."

* * * *

Rob's confidence impressed her. She hoped it would be that easy. She knew Manny was rattled by the threat.

They pulled in near the food truck and looked around. A few people wearing hats and gloves to ward off the chill were heading for the short line, but no one stood out as an older man accompanied by a lawyer.

"He might not even show," Rob said. "Whoever put him up to it could be satisfied they disrupted your business and cost you some customers."

Elise made a soft fist and hit her cupped hand. "That wouldn't solve anything. I still don't know why or who. That's the sticky part."

Rob reached for her hand. "Well, drats."

She burst out laughing. "Thank you."

He looked over her shoulder, through his side window. "Hate for you to lose that smile, but I think our target is about to appear as promised."

Elise followed his gaze and saw a man of about sixty and another man of about the same age, wearing a rumpled brown suit and overcoat, heading for her food truck. Her stomach did a somersault. "Let's go."

They intercepted the men. "Excuse me," she said. "I'm Elise Fayette. Half owner of this food truck. Are you the man who disrupted my business with an accusation of food poisoning?"

The casually-dressed man brought up his chin. "It's not just an accusation, it's true."

She kept focused on him. "And your name is?"

The man in the suit responded. "I'm his attorney. His name will be on the legal suit we intend to file if you refuse to settle by paying his emergency room bill. Until then you don't need to know his name in case you intend to harass him."

Elise folded her arms. "I'm speaking to your client. And I'm afraid I'll need his full name for my countersuit for slander. We also have no intention of paying his bill. There's no way that one out of over fifty tacos sold day before yesterday gave your client food poisoning. Not a single other person served that day has come forward with the same complaint. Unless your client tampered with it then ate it in order to shake us down with a fake claim."

She was on a roll. "Which begs another question. Where is he?"

The attorney's blinking increased. "Where's who?"

"The county health inspector. If your client was sick enough to go to the emergency room and have his stomach pumped, it would have to be reported immediately. My partner filed a preliminary report, but with no confirming report from a hospital, no action was taken. As you can see, we're open for business. No inspector showed up yesterday and none today. You, on the other hand can be reported for fraud."

"Multiple tacos are made at the same time," Rob added. "With the exact same ingredients. It would be pretty hard to taint one taco and not the rest. I have another question. Was that taco the only food he ate that day?"

She didn't understand Rob's question at first, then smiled. "Probably not. Can he prove some other food didn't cause his phantom food poisoning? Or maybe he has some pre-existing gastric issues he hasn't shared."

The *client* shook his head and took a step back, but before he spoke, Elise interrupted. "The answer is no. Do your worst and the answer is still no." She waved her finger back and forth, indicating the two men. "This doesn't even look real. Come back if you ever have any proof. If anything like this mess happens again, I'm pressing charges."

A thin girl came and stood near Rob. She wore a bright red hoodie with a quote printed on the front. **"You Matter – Unless you Multiply Yourself by the Speed of Light Squared – Then you Energy"** – Neil deGrasse Tyson

Elise huffed, still wound up after confronting the two men. "Um, this is a private conversation."

The girl bobbed her head and held out a mittened hand. "Sorry. I'm Deja." She waved at the others waiting in line. "We overheard this guy yesterday and wanted you to know several of us used to see him hanging around Theo's Tacos. It's a food truck about a quarter mile from here."

A small gasp escaped the unidentified client and Elise heard Rob chuckle. He reached for the girl's hand and shook it. "Thank you."

The girl's face nearly matched the color of her hoodie. "Any time."

The two older men have moved away and were talking in near whispers. The *attorney* glanced over his shoulder. "My client didn't want to ruin your reputation before allowing you to make things right. We'll be in touch." And they left.

Elise was nearly giddy. "Betcha they won't."

She walked to the truck window and leaned toward Manny. "I don't think he'll be back." She tipped her head toward the girl. "See the girl in the red hoodie? Free lunches for a week. On me."

Manny's daughter Angel piped up. "Thanks Elise. He's been crazy with worry. I told him it would turn out okay."

Elise stepped back. "Got business with my temporary partner. You guys take care."

She checked her watch. "That only took twenty minutes. Now, I'm all yours."

The look on his face made her pause. He actually looked like he wanted to take that as an up close and personal invitation. Why did she keep saying things like that? "Um, I'm freezing. Want to go to the truck and talk about next steps for the hunt?"

Rob rubbed his hands together. A neutral expression on his face. "Sounds good."

In the truck cab, he turned to her. "You okay?"

"Yes, thanks. And thanks for your help. You know. Backing me up."

He clicked the heat up a few notches. "Glad to be of service. You think maybe Theo's Taco Truck owner is the guy behind the sabotage attempts?"

Exactly what she thought. She and Rob made a good team. "You think so too?"

"It's a possibility."

Elise shifted a shoulder. "Bad timing, but that problem will have to come later. We need to concentrate on today's hunt if we want to maintain the lead."

Rob headed out of the parking lot. "Are we still going to North Meadows Park?"

"Best guess we have," Elise said. "Unless you thought of something better while we were helping those two liars on their way."

Chapter Seven

Rob forced his brain to stay on track. Elise smelled great. Like a field of flowers caught under an early snow. He shook his head. Wow. Maybe his years in Paris had left him open to seeing the nicer things around him. He slid a quick glance her way. Something he'd been doing a lot these past few days. Yep. She was still pretty, smart, and hard-working. No engagement ring, so there must be a catch. She had balked when he pulled out his plastic sheeting. Maybe she was really messy at home. He'd never seen her in anything but jeans and outdoor wear. Maybe she didn't own any heels and dressy dresses. Or, horrors. Maybe she doesn't balance her bank account every month either, you idiot. He laughed out loud.

They pulled into the park's lot. Not many cars. The snow wasn't deep enough to cancel school days or close businesses, so the grounds were almost empty.

Elise looked up from studying their sheets, now crumpled and creased. "Oh, we're here. It's a small place, so we can divide, walk each side of the perimeter looking for anything pointing north, and meet on the other side."

She made it hard. "Let's stick together. If we're alone and find the clue, we'll just have to go get the other person, then look for whoever signs it off."

Elise pulled her hair band into place and put on her mittens. "Right. Let's go."

A sign board close to the sidewalk showed the dimensions and seasonal interests. The park was shaped like a trapezoid and they were parked on the shortest side. Elise ran her mitten to the bottom. "Here we go. Seasonal displays are straight across, on the longest side, facing the main street."

Rob estimated the distance and noted their footwear. Both had on rubber ankle boots. He loved people who came prepared. "We could cut through to save some time. If this is as easy as we think, that may give us that extra minute we need to maintain the lead."

"With you," she said. "I think I see some colorful spots up front."

He squinted. She was right. He could pick out specks of bright colors among the trees across the grass and paths.

Elise lengthened her stride to match his longer one. "Come on. We need to make up for the side trip to my food truck."

They reached the display spot and Rob looked around, disappointed. No snowman. Just life-sized plastic carolers, a Christmas tree and stacks of presents. None of them pointing north.

"Good guess," Elise said. "But no win. The song's lyrics don't mention any of these things."

"Yeah. Too easy, I guess. Let's go back to the truck and crank up the heat. We can at least study our cheat sheets in comfort."

Elise looked around. "Agreed. Not a very balanced display, anyway. A big hole between the packages and the carolers."

They turned to see an older man coming toward them and struggling to keep a big pile of mainly white plastic from sliding off the side of a metal cart with small wheels he was dragging across the grass.

Rob hurried to him. "That looks heavy. Can I help?"

The man nodded. "Great if you could get the big guy. I've got the portable air compressor."

"What is this?" Rob asked.

"Oh. The snowman. His last year, I'm afraid. Probably be replaced by Santa next year. All the other pieces are hollow plastic and he's heavy vinyl filled with air. Found him on my drive-by this morning. Slow leak took him down and he's been in the shop being repaired for the last couple of hours. They're hoping it lasts the season."

Elise clapped. "Have you seen him fully inflated?"

He bounced a questioning look between the two of them. "Of course. North Meadow Park is part of my territory for the county parks department. Why'd you want to know?"

Rob grinned. "Thinking of bringing the kids down for pictures now that there's snow. Could you please show us what he looks like?" He caught a glimpse of Elise with her mouth partially open, but giving them kids was the best he could come up with. No rings necessary as they both had on gloves.

The older man shrugged. "Sure." He stood with a hand on his hip and one held in the air like he was waving. "Like this."

Rob picked up Elsie and twirled her around. "We were right and we almost missed it."

"Wait," she said. "Put me down, you wacko. If we *are* right, who signs off on the find?"

He saw the stupefied look on the face of the county parks worker. "Not him. He thinks we're nuts."

Their attention was drawn to a woman waving and calling, "Hello," from in front of a strip of small businesses across the street. She wore an apron with brown stains over jeans and a long-sleeved t-shirt. Ignoring caution, she sprinted toward them, stepping onto the sidewalk. "Hi. I'm a friend of Molly's. Are you two one of her scavenger hunt teams?"

"Yes," Rob said. "Thank you for finding us."

"Almost didn't," she replied, taking a piece of paper from her pocket. "I'm owner and chief barista for my shop over there. I came in at 6:00 and saw the snowman lying flat. I meant to call Molly but got busy filling a big order for a luncheon at a corporate office. I really didn't expect anyone to figure out her clue for a couple more hours. You guys are quick."

Which means either we're the first to get this song and clue, or have the best time. Either way it puts us ahead.

Elise held her hand out for the slip and put it in her pocket. "Thanks for your help. Much appreciated."

The woman rubbed her arms and watched for an opening in the traffic. "Sounds like fun. I already have my ticket to the gala. Good luck."

Elise gave a mitten wave and turned to Rob. "Ready."

They left a confused park employee filling the inflatable snowman with air and ran hand-in-hand back to Rob's truck.

Inside, he didn't want the day to end this early. "Where to? Lunch is your treat today."

Elise slapped the dash in a drum beat. "Fine with me. How about Theo's Taco Truck? I'm in the mood to continue our sleuthing success."

He was in the mood to continue being with her as long as she would tolerate him. "Great minds think alike. We can work on our research while we eat and watch the truck. Can't be as good as your tacos, though."

She snapped into her seatbelt. "Thank you, sir. Now, being on a winning team makes me hungry. Let's hit it."

Rob swung his hands up, index fingers pointing toward the windshield. "Yes, ma'am."

* * * *

Theo's Taco Truck being located a quarter mile from Elise and Manny's turned out to be a hunt of its own. They found it on a side street tucked between two parking lots. Not nearly as convenient as the prime place Elise's truck occupied, but close to more tech office buildings. One spot by the commercial dumpsters gave Rob his only parking option.

A youngish woman in a heavy brown jacket heaved up the lid to the dumpster and pushed in a big bag of garbage. She, and one guy waiting at the truck's order window, were the only two people besides he and Elise, in the lot. Instead of going back into one of the buildings, the woman in the brown coat went to the door of the truck cab and got in, turning the engine on.

Rob and Elise walked up behind the customer at the truck's window. When it was his turn, Rob asked for the taco and soft burrito combo.

"Make that two," Elise said. "Throw in a couple of colas. And I'm paying."

"Smells really good in there," Rob said to the guy at the window. "Are you Theo?"

The counter man sliced a quick look at the older man stationed at the grill, with his back to them. "Yeah, why?"

"No big deal," Elise said, handing through a debit card. "We had lunch at a competitor's taco truck yesterday and overheard the owner talking about being harassed and threatened. She mentioned tracking down a witness to a junker car sale. She told this guy if the harassment doesn't stop, she's going to get the police involved. You haven't had anything like that happen to you, have you?"

Theo ran her card, looking at the name, then passed it back. "Thanks. Just be a minute." And closed the window.

Rob watched him put the food into Styrofoam containers then into bags. He spoke low to Elise. "I think we found our food poisoning victim. At the grill."

She stood on tiptoe, trying to take a quick peek. "And maybe the female who called to cancel my produce orders. Are you sure it's the same older guy?"

"Almost positive. There's a strong resemblance."

The window slid open and the bag was passed out.

Rob handed it to Elise and took the two drinks. "Thanks."

No response from Theo as the window closed.

Elise held the warm bag close as they hurried to Rob's truck. "We did good. I wonder if these tacos have Theo's sauce on them?"

Rob clicked the locks on his truck as they approached. "You think he might be the other candidate for the sauce contract and somehow found out it was you? Or just a nasty taco truck competitor looking to sabotage a favored rival?"

She climbed into the cab, laughing as Rob cut off a chunk of plastic for their laps. "I think it's the latter and we put the fear of losing his license through a police investigation into him. And judging from his customer base, he's not my competition for the sauce contract."

He bit into the taco and made a face. "No blue-ribbon sauce here."

Elise took a bite and chewed slowly. "No. But there's a hint of duplication. The herbs are too weak, and the fish is too strong. Can't find a balance."

Rob concentrated on his next bite. She was right. She'd do well in an haute cuisine kitchen. "Needs more salt."

Elise started giggling. "At the very least." She dropped her taco on the plastic and picked up the burrito, giving it a suspicious inspection. "Where are we *really* having lunch?"

He mentioned a small sandwich shop and she started rolling up the plastic. "I love that place! Taco holiday. I want Panini!"

Her enthusiasm was contagious and his mouth watered. He could almost taste the Black Forest ham and Beecher's Flagship cheese. With avocado, and heirloom tomatoes on the side.

Elise dragged the plastic off his lap, rolled it in a ball and shoved it toward him. "Get moving before all the good stuff is gone."

Chapter Eight

Lunch over, Elise laced her fingers and stretched her arms forward, sighing. The small sandwich shop was nearly empty. Outside, the white-gray sky seemed low enough to touch. She sighed a second time. "As good as I remember, but I guess we'd better get our slip back to Aunt Molly."

"Yeah. Halfway through," Rob mused. "I'm going to miss running around, solving clues. You're a great partner whether we win or not."

Elise liked the emphasis he put on the word partner. Maybe after the holidays were over, she could take him out for a nice dinner and some recreational fooling around. She pulled up short. His smile of enjoyment made it look like he'd go for the same thing. "Oh, thank you. Same here."

Rob stood. "Thinking about adding hot sandwiches to the menu of my country French restaurant."

Elise followed suit. "Good idea." Then she noticed he'd taken the check. "Um, I'm sure I said this lunch was on me."

He hitched an eyebrow. "You paid for Theo's Tacos. Not my fault they needed salt. I've got this."

She stopped walking. "Noticed you're getting low on gas. You can buy lunch if I fill your tank."

He pulled his lips in and out. "Okay."

"Wait. What? You aren't going to argue?"

That smile of enjoyment took place again. "I plan to stay on your good side. That's the kind of guy I am."

Elise pinned him with a sharp look. "Heard that before."

"From who?"

"Are you asking me who said they plan to stay on my good side?"

Rob pulled his mouth down. "None of my business?"

She felt a rush of delight, but was now in a corner of her own making. She shifted a shoulder. "Long ago. Not important."

His eyes crinkled at her answer. "Good."

* * * *

The snow from the previous day was all but gone when Elise pulled into the Copper Circle lot shortly before ten the next morning. Her sleep-deprived brain took a disappointing hit when she didn't see Rob's truck. Oh, well. She would be spending the next four or five hours with him. Wait. That was too many. If they left for the hunt at ten, the goal remained to solve the clue and get signed off as soon as possible. But if she offered lunch again, she could stay in his company for at least another hour.

She jerked at a tap on her passenger door window. Franny Bostick stood outside motioning for her to open the door. Elise released the door lock and Franny slid into the car.

"You and Mr. Rob Culver are doing well in the competition."

Not known for her generosity, Franny had to be up to something, so Elise waited. She didn't have long.

"I wanted to let you in on a little secret," Franny said. "Sage Hill Bistro isn't the only restaurant business my family has invested in, locally. We will be signing the final financial agreement with very favorable terms for your partner's new place, next week."

Elise could practically hear the other shoe dropping. "That *is* interesting. So, you're thinking if Rob and I win and cater the gala, his reputation will be enhanced and your family will get a return on their investment that much sooner."

Franny flattened her lips. "What I'm thinking, is that my own reputation is new and could use a boost. If you do win, and for some reason are unable to partner with Mr. Culver for the gala, your little start-up catering business might find itself with a handy cash infusion that could be used for marketing or other resources. No strings attached."

Wow. The bribe couldn't be plainer. She put on her best serious expression. "Still three days left. You and Gareth may win yet. But you've made good points. Let me think about your offer."

At the mention of her partner's name, Franny made a decidedly sour face then cut a glance at the winery driveway. She reached for her door handle. "My offer won't stay open for long."

Rob waited for Elise on the steps to the tasting room. "You thinking about a new partner?"

"No, but she is. I'll tell you later."

The other two teams were already inside and her Aunt Molly was behind the tasting counter.

Franny Bostick raked her gaze over Rob like he was Thanksgiving leftovers.

Molly held up her clipboard and three envelopes. "Day three results are in ladies and gentlemen. It's still anybody's win. Three points to team one, two points to team three, and one point to team two." She looked at each pair in turn. "Here's an interesting fact, and one to remember. Only twelve minutes difference between first and second place for yesterday."

Elise walked over, took the envelope labeled Team Three, tore it open and read the contents. She smiled like today's clue was in the bag. Rob returned her smile and they left. Her giggle escaped halfway to his truck.

"Good work," he said. "I heard two gasps and one harsh whisper." He leaned over her shoulder. "Here Comes Santa Claus is the song and reindeer snacks is the clue."

She read it a second time. "Easy peasy, right? I wonder if one of the other teams has already solved this one? After coming in second yesterday, we need to get hot on it."

Rob frowned and clicked the truck doors unlocked. "Easy peasy? Really? I'm glad you think so. Neither of us had this song on our lists."

Elise huffed a breath as they slid inside. "No idea. I'm just trying to stay positive. Made the decision to bow out of the sauce competition last night so I'm more or less sleep deprived. I also feel bad about the times turned in yesterday. We lost a point by twelve minutes. If we hadn't stopped at Theo's Taco truck to snoop for twenty minutes, we would have won the three points instead of two."

He rubbed the back of her neck. "Um, glad you came to that decision. We're going to be very busy. Also, is this short memory of yours genetic?"

What is he talking about? "You lost me."

"If we'd arrived twenty minutes earlier, we'd have missed the park employee with the deflated snowman and the lady barista who'd been too busy with her large order. So, you actually got us two points instead of none. Which keeps us in the lead."

"Oh. Happy accident, I guess. Had a lot on my brain lately."

"Anything I can do?"

She could think of a few replies that included cuddling but settled for something less obvious. "Pat my hand and say, 'Who's a good girl?' "

"I can do you one better," he said, sliding his arm across the back of her seat and pulling her in for a hug. "Who's a good girl?"

Damn seatbelt. She leaned in and swallowed a moan of satisfaction. Really nice way to start a day. Until . . . Gareth and Franny drove past the front of Rob's truck and stared through the windshield. Yes, it was cold outside, but Franny's look managed to drop the temperature another five degrees.

"Team one's getting an eyeful."

Rob broke the hug and noticed Gareth's car. "Bother you?"

Elise gave him a frank stare despite the wobble of her stomach. "Nobody's business but ours."

He kissed her temple and leaned back. "That works for me."

Boy, did that work for her. "Me too. And speaking of work. Since neither of us has any ready ideas, we should start by googling the song lyrics. See if we can associate any key words with our clue."

They pulled out their cell phones, but Elise could barely concentrate. Rob Culver had everything. Mad skills in the kitchen, good looks, smarts, ambition. An unattached flirt?

Rob nudged her arm with his elbow. "Elise?"

"Cookies."

"We're trying to come up with clues in the lyrics. Are you hungry?"

She shook her head. "The clue is reindeer snacks. Vixen and Blitzen are two of Santa's reindeer. The snacks that might put the two together are reindeer cookies. All I've got right now."

Rob looked completely blank.

Elise sighed. "A round cookie, mini chocolate chips for eyes, candy red hot for the nose, break a small pretzel in half for the antlers. Attach everything with caramel. Lots of different recipes but they all look like reindeer cookies."

"Brilliant. I'm game. Where do we find these cookies and Santa?"

"Redmond Town Center has a cookie shop. Good as any place to start. And there are Santa look-a-likes at most of the malls this time of year. We should be able to make it there in under a quarter hour."

* * * *

Rob congratulated himself. He'd been wanting to get closer to Elise. Feel those shiny curls against his cheek. She'd even leaned in, which meant she was interested too. He hoped. And he really wanted them to win. It would mean more time together, planning the menu and the rest of the myriad of details involved in catering a large event.

He glanced at her when he took the next right. She looked nervous. He hoped she wasn't regretting his hug. Maybe if he changed the subject. "You said you have a lot on your mind. Are you being harassed by whoever's got it in for your taco truck?"

"Oh. No. Remember I said I'd tell you about Franny's visit to my car?"

His heart sank. "Yes. Something about a new partner. I think it's too late to switch."

"*I* don't want to switch," Elise said. "But Franny has an idea how she can hedge her bets. A win, win, win. By changing partners after the contest is over."

"How?"

"You probably noticed she has no faith in, or fondness for, Gareth."

Rob thought he and Elise were paired well, like red wine with a simple, but great, cut of steak. "Might be one of the reasons we're ahead."

Elise nodded. "She told me your new restaurant has investors. One of whom is her family. So, if we happen to win the contest, and for whatever reason I'm unable to partner with you for the gala, she could step in. Your investor money would be safe, her reputation would get a boost, and my start-up catering service would become eligible for a cash infusion. No strings attached."

He pulled over and turned off the truck. "Did you agree?"

Elise frowned. "Of course not. Don't be an idiot. I told her I'd have to think about it. Which I have no intention of doing. Why? Are you interested?"

Rob answered her by pulling her in for another hug. "Not in the least." He leaned back and made direct eye contact. "My overwhelming interest right now is sitting next to me. As far as Franny's threat to have her family's investment withdrawn, I couldn't care less. The consortium they're part of has less than eighteen percent. And the only reason they have any interest at all is because a friend of mine is the primary and he doesn't do that kind of deal."

Elise sighed. A look of relief on her face. "I don't know why I let her get in my head or how much she wants to offer me, but my answer's the same as yours."

Add guts or self-confidence, whatever, to the rest of her attributes, and Rob couldn't help himself. He took her shoulders gently and drew her in for a quick kiss. "Thanks."

She tilted her head and smiled. "Not that that wasn't nice. Very nice. But, if we're going to win the hunt, we have two more days to score. Starting with reindeer snacks."

Two teenage boys honked and gave them a thumbs up as they drove by in the opposite direction. Rob laughed. "Let 'em get their own girls."

"Slow down," Elise said. "You haven't got your own girl, yet. We've known each other three and a half days."

He turned on the truck and pulled away from the curb, looking through the windshield. "I'm a decisive man."

The Redmond Town Center three weeks before Christmas was abuzz with shoppers. They finally secured a parking spot and made their way to the cookie store. The selection was amazing. Santas, elves, sleighs, stars, bells, and yes, reindeer, filled the shiny glass shelves.

The girl behind the counter smiled at him. "May I help you?"

"I believe you can," he said. "We're a scavenger hunt team looking for specific reindeer snacks. We were hoping your reindeer-shaped cookies would get us the sign-off we need to win today."

Her smile faded. "Sign-off?"

Rob's optimism faded too. "Yes. When we reach the right clue, there is someone nearby who signs off for us to verify that we found it."

The girl's expression didn't change. "My manager's out to lunch until, whenever."

"So, I guess these aren't the reindeer snacks we need," he said. "But thanks anyway."

He turned to Elise. "Drats."

She stopped the girl. "Do you know if any other shops here at the center sell reindeer cookies?"

The counter girl shrugged. "I don't think so."

Heavy sigh from Elise. "Back to the truck to puzzle this out?"

Inside the cab, Rob tapped the side of his thumb on the steering wheel. "Okay. The basics. What do we need to know about reindeer and snacks?"

"Good," Elise said. "Since the reindeer aren't the snacks, at least here. Then they're eating them. Hence, live reindeer. Agreed?"

Rob nodded. "We live in an urban area, but people who live in areas like Enumclaw have deer and elk sightings. Maybe a farmer supplements their food with corn or something."

"Right thought process, but I think we need Santa or something Christmassy in the mix. Besides, wandering around

Enumclaw knocking on doors to ask if they are feeding the wildlife isn't something Molly would have us do."

He turned on his truck, adjusting the heat. "If we're sticking with live reindeer, where do we find them? I mean are there any Santa with sleigh and reindeer enactments or photo opportunities, something like that?"

Elise slapped her hands on her thighs bouncing in her seat. "Head for Issaquah. I think I've got it."

Rob stared at her.

"Earth to Rob," she said. "Why aren't you driving? I'll check to see if they're open, GPS the address, and explain while you're driving."

He put the car in gear and headed out. *What had he missed? Never mind. Her intuition had been spot-on so far.*

She finished with her phone and turned in her seat. "Good news, bad news. I think our clue is at Cougar Mountain Zoo in Issaquah. They bring in live reindeer during the Christmas season. The kids can meet Santa, sit in a sleigh, and feed the reindeer. It's got all the components. Plus, Molly lives in Issaquah. Has for years."

"Got it," he said. "And the bad news is, so would Will and Jos since they were raised there. Unless they already worked this on Tuesday, when they got first place."

Elise nodded. "Very possible. I thought of it because Aunt Molly took all the family kids there when we were little." She turned up the volume on her phone. "We should be there in under twenty minutes."

Chapter Nine

Elise had forgotten how much she'd enjoyed coming to this conservation zoo and park. The animals and birds looked well-cared for and healthy. She headed for the large reindeer corral.

"I like this place," Rob said. "Let's stop on the way out. I want to make a donation."

"Works for me. We should probably check with the guy who takes care of the reindeer first."

They approached the corral and watched a pair of towheaded kids throwing in snacks for the two enclosed reindeer. Elise leaned over the fence and shouted into the barn. "Hello. Anybody there?"

An older man came out with a handful of hay and pointed. "You can buy the deer food up that way."

Elise waved. "We're a scavenger hunt team and think your reindeer snacks are one of our clues. Is there someone we can talk to about it?"

He spread the hay on the ground, pulled a walkie-talkie from his belt holster and made a call. After listening to the response, he shrugged and disconnected. "Mrs. Jensen will be down in a minute. She said something about filling out paperwork."

Rob picked her up and swung her around. "We did it."

The older man's gaze landed everywhere but on them, so he went back into the barn.

Elise stepped back from Rob's embrace, smiling. "I hope we did."

"Generous of you to agree it's we. Since you've come up with all of the right answers."

She shook her head. "Not the way partnerships work. At least with me. For instance, Manny loves the thrill behind the grill and engaging the public. So, I order the produce for delivery, dabble in recipes, do the books and we take turns scrubbing the truck inside and out on the weekend."

Elise fisted her hands on her hips. "Your contribution to our team consists of punctuality, driving safely, being agreeable, taking window duty in our taco truck, helping me deal with those guys from Theo's Taco truck, and more. All in all, I think we're pretty even."

Rob dragged his mouth to one side. "I sound like an overachieving Uber driver."

She hadn't mentioned anything personal, not really. *Did he mean he wanted her to?*

Before the opportunity presented itself and she could fashion an answer, it passed, as a woman bundled in a denim hoodie lined in flannel approached.

She held out a slip of paper to Elise. "Hi. I'm Madeline Jensen. You two made pretty good time. Not as good as the first team, but close."

Since she didn't say anything about a second team and it was Thursday, that probably meant the last team would get this clue tomorrow. Not an easy one to solve. It was mean, but she hoped it would go to Franny and Gareth.

"Thank you," Rob said and squeezed her hand.

Mrs. Jensen pulled her neck into her jacket and smiled, turning. "Good luck."

"Wait," he said, pulling out his wallet and picking out twenty dollars. "Can you see to it this goes into the donation kitty?"

Mrs. Jensen took the cash, a big smile lighting her face. "You bet. Thanks so much."

Elise looked at her and Rob's joined hands. "Four down, one to go. Come on, overachiever."

Rob laughed. "I've been counting in my head. We should get two or three points for today. If we do, we'd have to get a zero or a one for tomorrow's clue to lose."

"I have every intention of winning."

He stopped walking. "I accepted this scavenger hunt challenge thinking we would be tasked to find some gourmet peppermint bark or a rare Chinese herb. Food-related clues.

The top team would cater the gala. Instead, I found you. I've already won."

Elise's nerves prickled across her shoulders and up her neck. Just four days, and emotional insanity had overtaken her. Well, not just her. Apparently, Rob was infected, too. But he certainly deserved a response. She studied those beautiful eyes. "I'm not a hundred percent sure if what we're feeling is the real thing or whether getting thrown together in . . ."

He pulled her into his arms, lowered his head and kissed her.

The kiss left her weak-kneed. "Maybe."

"What?"

Still wrapped in his arms, Elise opened her eyes. Wait. Had she said 'maybe,' out loud? "Um, just wondering if maybe this is a response to all the craziness we're going through. You know, after the gala, and new restaurant for you and more catering business for me. And I forgot to say Manny is talking about us buying another truck . . ."

"Doesn't matter," Rob said. He stepped back. "None of it. Unless you want it to."

Elise paused. Normally she was a cautious, linear, step by step thinker, weighing the pros and cons. Not this time. Not with Rob.

He rubbed her arms. "Am I wrong?"

"No, you're not. I'm every bit as crazy about you. It's that I feel like I'm being towed under. We know next to nothing about each other."

That smile that was beginning to fade, bloomed again. "Easy. I pay my taxes, have no homicidal tendencies, no wacko ex's, my parents love me, and genes that will more than likely produce tall children . . . both of them."

Elise started laughing. "Sold." She meant to seal it with a hug, but Rob pulled her in for another amazing kiss.

He took her hand and walked toward his truck. "Start thinking about the menu for the gala. We're going to win."

"Didn't I say something like that earlier?"

"Yes, But I was distracted."

They got into his truck. "Since we made another stop before coming here," Rob said. "We might not get the three points. What do you think?"

Elise nodded. "If Jos's team pairings had stuck, each team would've had someone on it that had come here as a kid. That was probably Aunt Molly's original intent. Since Franny and Gareth got one point on Tuesday's puzzle, this might have been it. Franny is new to the area and neither of them seems like the type to visit zoo conservation parks."

Rob turned on the truck. "Okay. I did the math. First, I think Will and Jos are out of the running. They only have five points and would need two threes to pull it out. So, if we make three points for today's puzzle, that would give us ten out of fifteen with one day to go. If, on the other hand, Gareth and Franny get the three points, we would be dead even for first place. Tomorrow would determine the winner."

"Not the end of the world if we came in second," she said. "But I would sure like to thumb my nose at Franny Bostick."

Rob pulled her to him and kissed the end of her nose. "Take that, Franny Bostick."

Elise sighed a happy sigh. Three days ago, she was single and busy and not looking. Today, Rob Culver was talking permanence. She needed to keep her head on straight. It all seemed like a daydream. *But I could sure get used to his hugs and kisses on a regular basis.* "What now? It's barely lunch time."

"Paninis again?"

She tipped her head. "For a guy who plates some of the best haute cuisine in the Pacific Northwest, you sure like middle class food."

"Not really," he said. "Life's too short to settle. What I like is anything that's made well. Your tacos, a great burger, or the aforementioned paninis."

Elise could think of one more thing that was made well. And wondered why someone hadn't snapped him up. "Paninis would be fine."

On the short drive, second and third thoughts began piling up. When they arrived, Elise put her hand on his arm. "I've been thinking."

He sighed. "So've I."

"I mean, the physical is amazing," she said. "And as much as I know about you, I like. A lot. I just feel caught in an undertow."

Rob took her hand. "Let me explain." His gaze found something over her shoulder, then reconnected. "My passion has always been food. Outside of my time studying in France, I haven't traveled. I have no hobbies, I don't date. My world is pretty small. But when I find something I like; I tend to go overboard. And fast."

He continued. "I don't mean crazy possessive, or mental." He smiled. "I promise."

Her stomach unclenched. "Then baby steps?"

"Sure. If that's what you want. Right now, I'm starving and I think it's my turn to buy."

Chapter Ten

Rob learned a lot during lunch. They had similar values and interests. Elise had eclectic taste in furniture and had shown him pictures of some pieces she'd refinished. She had also traveled. Places he'd thought about, but never taken the time to visit. It was a new, but comfortable experience.

They dropped off their time slip. Neither of the other teams was there and Molly wouldn't say if they had already been in. Rob walked Elise to the parking lot. "I'm sure we racked up a two or three. If we both come up with menu ideas for the gala, we can be that much better prepared." She laughed and pulled his head down for a kiss. "Will do."

He raised an eyebrow and tugged her in for a hug. "Um, maybe our time could be better spent in other pursuits."

"Menu pursuit was your idea," she said and chucked him under the chin before getting in her car and driving away.

Rob threw back his head and laughed. He'd found something, make that someone, who interested him more than food. Hot damn.

* * * *

Ten a.m. the next day brought continued cold weather and overcast skies. Clouds that matched the mood of the group gathered at Copper Circle. Will and Jos looked the most down-in-the-mouth and Rob had to work hard at keeping his grin under control when he saw Elise.

"Hi," he said. "Did you sleep well?"

She returned his cheerful grin. "Not at all. Pursued menus all night. Got real excited."

Molly walked to the counter. "Last day, teams. First, for yesterday's points. Three points to team one, two points to team three and one point to team two. That makes teams one and three even at nine points apiece. Today's puzzle will be the decider. Second and third place teams won't miss out altogether, however. Their names will be mentioned on the entrance placards at the gala."

She continued, holding out the envelopes. "Here are your puzzles for today. Good luck, all."

Rob tore the envelope open and handed the sheet to Elise. She smiled. " 'All I want for Christmas is You,' is the song. The clue is 'herb of the month. Think scentless Christmas candle.' Wow. I got nothin'."

He shrugged. "Want to sit in here where's it's warm and work on it? There's hot apple cider. My treat."

Elise took off her jacket and mittens and sat on the bench around the firepit re-reading their puzzle for the day.

Rob wracked his brain, because he knew a lot about herbs but wasn't big on candles. All he could come up with was cranberry and bayberry, or balsam and cedar which were all scented.

He drummed his fingers on the counter. Behind it was a wall display of holiday items for sale. Small wreaths made of wine corks, bits of mistletoe tucked into cellophane bags and tied with a red ribbon, Santa hats to fit wine bottles and tall, Christmas gift bags meant to hold wine bottles, were artfully arranged. Molly slid two steaming glass mugs filled with amber liquid toward him. "Enjoy."

He carried the drinks to Elise and sat next to her. "Got anything?"

She shook her head. "Those scentless candles with the batteries and fake wicks can be purchased in lots of places. You can also buy soy or wax candles without scent. Again, in lots of places. The herb of the month thing has me stumped. You're the expert there."

Rob nodded and sipped his apple cider. "Yeah. Most of the herbs I work with are hothouse. You can buy them fairly fresh year-round. I also have several in pots in my kitchen. I've never heard of an herb of the month."

"Maybe we're thinking too big," Elise said. "Let's scale it back, word by word. I googled the lyrics while you were getting the drinks. Thank you, by the way. This is delicious. Anyhow, here are the keywords that got my attention." She handed him a list written on the back of one of her pages.

He skimmed the words. Presents, wish, stocking, tree, fireplace, toy, snow, mistletoe, North Pole, Saint Nick, reindeer, sleigh bells, and Santa. Most of which were included in a number of Christmas songs.

"Any jump out at you?" she asked.

Rob really wanted those last three points. He wanted them more for Elise than himself. Herb of the month? Okay. Assuming the month was December, nothing on the list was an herb he was familiar with. He pulled out his cell phone and googled the only possibility, mistletoe. He read the information, then turned around and grinned at Molly. She smiled and bobbled her eyebrows. "Something on your mind?"

Elise twisted. Her gaze bouncing between Rob and her Aunt Molly. "What's going on?"

Rob pulled her to her feet. "*We are*. We are going on to cater the gala. I just solved today's puzzle." He turned toward the counter. "How about it, Mrs. Daughter? Do we have the record for this one?"

She looked at her watch. "Fourteen minutes. I'd say so. And call me Molly. We'll be working closely together."

Elise fisted hands on her hips. "Will somebody tell me what's happening? Rob, did you really solve it?"

"About time, right? Yes. Google and I solved it. Did you know mistletoe is an herb? Did you know if you squeezed out the oil and put it in a candle, there would be no scent?"

"Um, no, and no. So the mistletoe in the puzzle is right here?"

He pointed to the wall behind the counter where Molly held up their signed-off slip.

Elise clapped. "Sneaky."

Rob stepped forward to take the slip. "You won't regret it."

Molly Daughter smiled. "On the contrary. You two have earned it."

* * * *

Elise couldn't stop smiling. Another Copper Circle wine club member just asked for a business card. Hot off the presses and given to her by Rob earlier in the kitchen. She pulled a card out of her black silk waistcoat pocket and peeked at it again.

Culver and Fayette Catering 425.555.2733.

She had withdrawn from putting her red sauce on the market during the two weeks leading up to the gala. Their tireless investment in time, energy, and combination of skills ensured the event was proving a big success. At least she'd thought so until Rob had opened the box with the newly minted cards and handed her one. She'd wondered out loud at so few left inside. "Fifty is the minimum number they'd print," he'd explained.

"Oh," was all she'd said, her head down. *Minimum.*

"I'll kick it up to five hundred when we make it Culver and Culver," Rob had replied and pulled her into a hug. "I can wait about six months. Can I get a yes for a June wedding?"

She kissed him warmly. "Of course. But who will we get to cater it?"

The End

Author Bio

DeeAnna is a freelance editor and travel agent for happy endings (romantic suspense, women's fiction, children's picture books and mysteries). She writes and teaches for the love of it, has never met a dog she did not want to pet, or a pie she did not want to taste. She tries to live life without props.

Other Titles by this author

Published by The Wild Rose Press

Gambling on the Goddess

McCarren's Rules ~ Angel Falls

Self-Published

Beach Reads (anthology)

Delta on my Mind

Chasing Glory

Ellori's Fine Adventure

The Crown of Everything